wicked winemakers
CENTRAL COAST
FIRST LABEL
—BOOK FOUR—

ZIN'S Sins

HEATHER SLADE

Table of Contents

1

Jada

My wrists burned as the rope he'd used to tie me to the hooks he'd pounded into the wall chafed my skin. I was bound facing him so I could witness his pain, he'd said, because I was there instead of the woman he really wanted.

"I told you to open your fucking eyes!" he screamed like he repeatedly did before he cracked the whip that, seconds later, would slice into my naked flesh.

I clenched my jaw, opening my eyes as wide as I could, knowing if they were closed when the strands of leather connected with my body, he'd make me endure several more lashes, worse than the first.

"*Jada. Wake up.* You're having a nightmare," I heard a deep voice say in the split second before the whip hit.

Nightmare? I squinted through one eye, then opened both to look into those of my brother.

"Montano?" I tried to whisper, but no sound came out.

He touched my forehead with a cool, damp cloth. My stomach rolled with the pungent smell of pine and lemon, but the nausea subsided when he caressed my cheek with his other hand. "It was just a dream. You're safe, sis. I've got you."

My eyes darted around the room. I heard the steady beep of a machine, but when I tried to turn my head to see it, I found I was unable to move. I wanted to ask where I was, but I couldn't form the words. When was the last time I had? All I remembered was every time I'd opened my mouth, it was to scream.

When Montano glanced behind me, I tried to turn my head a second time. Again, it wouldn't move. Not that I really needed to look. I knew Vaile Oliver—Zin—sat on the other side of the bed. I always knew when he was close. In the past, I'd craved it. I didn't now.

The door opened, and a man walked in. I recognized him, though I didn't know him well. *Bones*—that's what my brother and his friends called him. He was a doctor.

Montano, who those same friends called Onyx, stood and leaned down to kiss my forehead. "I'll be right outside." I tried to nod, but I couldn't. It was as though my brain and body were disconnected.

The pine-and-lemon aroma of the cloth he'd held was replaced by the sterile stench of bleach on the bed's linens. Why was my sense of smell heightened to the point where it nauseated me?

I watched Bones check the leads of the machines attached to my skin and smelled the antiseptic on his hands blending with the disinfectant, but I still couldn't feel his touch. I couldn't fucking feel *anything*. Did that mean I was dreaming? Was what Montano had said was a nightmare my reality, or was this?

"Luisa is here," said Bones.

Luisa. My best friend. The woman the lunatic had wanted instead of me. I'd heard him tell her—or some-one—I'd demanded he trade me for her. I knew Luisa. Once she found out he had me, she'd do everything she could to get me out of his clutches, even if it meant sacrificing herself.

Bones studied me. "I can let her know you're not ready for visitors."

I tried again and was able to shake my head enough for him to notice. He nodded and left the room.

"Jada?" Zin reached over and stroked my hair. Like with Bones, I could smell the bodywash he'd used and the scent of his shampoo. I could see his hand move but couldn't feel it. I closed my eyes, wondering again if I was dreaming.

"Sweetheart, Luisa is here," Zin whispered a few seconds later.

My eyes met hers, and without thinking about it, I raised my hand. I studied its movement as though it belonged to someone other than me.

"Leave us," I whispered like Zin had, stunned and relieved when the words came out.

Zin stood, leaned down, and kissed my forehead like my brother had before walking out the door Luisa had come through.

I flinched when her hand rested on mine, not because it hurt, but because it was the first of another's touch I could feel. My eyes filled with tears. "I didn't"—God, my throat hurt. Was it from screaming?—"ask him to trade." I managed to finish my thought, but every word I uttered felt like sandpaper on my larynx.

She held my hand between both of hers. "Oh, sweetheart, I know you didn't. I know you would never."

I rested my head against the pillow. "He…he…"

"Shh," she soothed. "We don't have to talk about it now, Jada. We don't ever have to talk about it unless you want to."

I closed my eyes and focused on the slow beep of the machine I'd heard when I first woke up, matching each breath I took to its rhythm, wondering if I'd ever be able to speak of the hours I spent held captive by a madman.

If I could, would anyone want to hear my story? I hadn't wanted to hear Luisa's. "I'm sorry." I peered at her through tears as her own flooded her eyes.

"There's nothing for you to be sorry for, Jada."

She was wrong, not that I could admit the real reason why I'd apologized. When she returned to the States after being rescued from a shipping container along with several other human trafficking victims, I'd told her we didn't need to talk about it right away. It hadn't been to ease her pain. It was to protect myself from feeling it.

"I'm the one who's sorry. He wanted me," she whispered. "God, Jada, can you ever forgive me?"

I wanted to reassure her like she had me, but the words wouldn't come. Instead, I stared at my hand, studying where the plastic tube disappeared into the hole in my flesh, delivering fluids into my body. Why could I feel her touch, but not it? Why could I turn my head, even raise my arm, but not *feel* it? Even my torso—where I'd been repeatedly whipped—was numb. *Why?*

"I need to rest," I said, pulling my hand from hers.

Her brow furrowed, and her eyes scrunched. "Um, sure. Of course."

I turned away, knowing if I didn't, I'd beg her to stay, beg her to comfort me, even though when she was the one in pain, I hadn't been able to do that for her.

From the corner of my eye, I saw her stand. "Do you want me to ask Zin to come back in?"

I closed my eyes and nodded, willing the tears not to fall until after she left the room.

"Jada? Are you—"

"Please go," I whispered.

2

Zin

"I killed the motherfucker," I admitted, looking into the eyes of my closest friend.

"I would've done the same thing," said Press, who was like a brother to me. "It's in the hands of law enforcement now," he added, his voice low like mine was.

"You may be right, but if the other *sonuvabitch*—the one I know Hamad Al Zaabi was working with—is ever let out of prison, I'll hunt him down and torture him far worse than he did Jada. Then I'll kill him."

When questioned, Manual Varilla, the human trafficker who'd originally abducted Luisa, swore he had no idea who had Jada. I knew in my gut he was lying.

"We'll kill him together," said Press under his breath, raising his head when Luisa slipped out of where Jada lay in a makeshift hospital room.

It had been set up for triage on Butler Ranch two years ago when a fire raged out of control on the vineyard property and several workers were injured.

Doc Butler, one of the men on the rescue team, was a physician's assistant. After I'd carried Jada to the waiting Akicita helicopter and he'd determined her injuries weren't life-threatening, he made the call to bring her here. I still wasn't certain it was the right decision, even after he and Onyx, who was also in the helicopter with us, assured me it was.

"Jada asked for you," said Luisa, whose tear-filled eyes mirrored my own.

I squared my shoulders and was on my way back in when I felt her hand on my arm. "I hope you can get through to her, Zin."

Rather than turn the knob and open the door, I let go and leaned against the wall. I didn't need to ask Luisa what she meant. I'd seen it firsthand. It was as though someone else inhabited Jada's body—a ghost in a broken shell rather than the spirited, vibrant, vital woman who'd left my bed yesterday morning.

Jada asking for me now was a good sign. It meant she was talking, something that, until a few minutes ago, she hadn't done other than to whisper for me to leave her and Luisa alone.

I opened the door, eased it closed behind me, and approached the bed. When I brushed the hair from her forehead, she flinched as though my touch had scorched her flesh. Almost worse, her eyes wouldn't meet mine.

"Jada?"

"Don't."

Don't what? Touch her? I landed in the chair as much as sat. I couldn't touch the woman I'd taken another's life in order to save? The woman I'd held in my arms and carried out of the place where a madman had strung her up against a wall and repeatedly whipped and tortured her?

"Luisa said you asked me to come in."

Her gaze was downcast, and she shook her head. "I want to be left alone."

"Would you at least look at me?"

"I don't want you here."

"What did I—"

"Get out!" she spat, clutching her throat. The hatred I saw in her eyes when she finally looked into mine for longer than a couple of seconds baffled me.

"What the fuck did I do?"

"You killed him."

"You're damn right I did. *In order to save your life.*"

"Leave, Zin."

"Fuck that. Talk to me, Jada."

She closed her eyes and turned her head so she faced the wall instead of me, but I didn't move. I couldn't.

The door opened, and Onyx poked his head in. "We need to talk," he whispered.

I nodded, leaned over, and kissed Jada's cheek. I didn't give a shit whether she hated that I had.

"Let's take this outside, son," Onyx said when I followed him down the hallway.

He and I were the same age. We'd gone to high school together. Calling people son, or dude or sis or whatever, was a quirk of his. But for those who knew him well, they'd learned what he called you was indicative of the conversation to come.

"What's this about, Onyx?"

I'd barely said his name when I felt his fist connect with my face. I stumbled against the pillar of the front porch, as stunned that I hadn't seen it coming as I was from the radiating pain. I wiped at the blood spewing from my nose with the back of my hand and bent at the waist when vertigo threatened to put me on my ass.

"What the fuck, *son*?" I shot back at him.

I heard him walking toward me, but didn't straighten until he was almost toe-to-toe with me. I stood upright and put my hands on my hips, leaving them there even when he poked his finger into my chest.

"You were reckless," he seethed.

"I saved Jada's life. You should be thanking me, asshole."

"You and your little vigilante group are dangerous. Why were you even there in the first place? You had no business inserting yourself into a planned op."

I opened my mouth, then closed it. When we first started seeing each other, Jada and I had agreed to keep our relationship secret. I hadn't even told Press about us until yesterday, and I doubted she'd confided in anyone either. Until I could speak to her about whether that had changed, I couldn't confess the reason I was there to anyone.

When I didn't respond, he continued. "You're untrained, undisciplined, and irresponsible. Until now, I let you play your game, but no more. If it's the last thing I do, I'll shut you motherfuckers down."

"You don't know what you're talking about."

Onyx stepped even closer, his nose almost touching my still-bleeding one. "You finally went too far, son."

"He would've killed her."

"If you hadn't been where you shouldn't have, we would've taken him down alive. Instead of one dead trafficker, we would've had the chance to take down the entire ring."

"Like with Varilla?" I knew it was the wrong thing to say before I said it, but I didn't care. As Press and I had discussed, the man knew far more than he was willing to confess, and no one had managed to get it out of him.

Onyx got right back in my face. "Stay away from Jada. You don't even so much as look at her, or I'll end you, Oliver. Don't think I fucking won't." He stalked inside, slamming the front door behind him.

I dragged my forearm across my face, sat on a porch step, and put my head in my hands.

The hothead in me wanted to get in my car and throw gravel as I peeled out the ranch's gate. It's what I always did when I felt backed into a corner. This time, though, something more important than my pride was at stake. This time, Jada mattered more to me than me. I was ashamed to admit, even to myself, how rare that was.

I stiffened when I heard the door open and footfalls that had to belong to a man approached me. Doc sat on the step. "Is it broken?" he asked as I continued wiping the blood away as it streamed from my nose.

I shrugged.

"At the very least, we should pack it."

"I figured you came out to finish where he left off."

Doc looked out at the vineyards. "I'm plenty mad at you, Zin, but now isn't the time for us to hot wash it. Jada is our priority." He stood. "Come with me."

I followed him into the house, avoiding eye contact with everyone we passed as he led me into the kitchen.

"Guess he told you," I said, looking at the items laid out on the table.

"Onyx is pissed, not heartless."

"He said he'd kill me if I so much as looked at his sister."

"Like I said, he's pissed."

"Are you sure bringing her here rather than to the hospital was the right decision?" I asked.

"Jada's wounds were caused by a cat o' nine tails. There are some lacerations. However, the majority of them are not deep. Some required stitches, but not all. Our main concern now is preventing infection."

"You didn't answer my question, Doc."

He nodded. "I based my decision on the factors I just explained to you. When we were in the Akicita, you also heard Onyx say Jada has never been in a hospital. The fact that we'd be taking her to a place where we'd have limited access to her, along with considering that law enforcement would've gotten involved after she was admitted, made me certain bringing her here was for the best." He shoved a large piece of tightly rolled cotton up one nostril.

"*Fuck!* Was that really necessary?"

"You know as well as I do there may be others working with Hamad Al Zaabi and Manual Varilla. Jada's and Luisa's safety were a factor in my decision as well."

Again, he hadn't answered my last question. However, when he shoved the second wad up my other nostril, I decided I'd be better off keeping my mouth shut.

"There you are," said Press, joining us in the kitchen. When he walked around Doc and saw my face, his eyes opened wide. "Jesus, what happened?"

"Onyx's fist."

"Is it broken?" he asked like Doc had.

"Yes," the other man answered for me. "You'll need to change the dressings every few hours. More are in this bag." He handed it to me. "It's probably going to hurt like hell, not that you don't deserve it."

"Hey, I thought you said you weren't heartless."

"I said Onyx wasn't, and believe me, shoving that wad of cotton up your nose could've hurt a fuck of a lot worse."

When he left the kitchen, I pulled out a chair and sat down. "She kicked me out."

Press pulled out the chair beside me. "Jada?"

"She told me she wanted me to leave. When I asked why, she said it was because I killed Al Zaabi."

He motioned to my face. "The same reason Onyx broke your nose is my guess."

I leaned in closer to him. "That wasn't all. He threatened to take down Los Caballeros."

Press leaned back. "Not the first time we've received such a threat."

"It is the first time someone has enough proof of our existence to be successful." I put my head in my hands. "I know I fucked up, Press, but Al Zaabi was going to kill her."

He rested his hand on my shoulder. "I can't say one way or another whether someone on the K19 team would've been able to neutralize him before he did or not. We'll never know. However, Jada is alive, and that is what truly matters. When things settle down, Doc, Onyx, and the rest of their team will come to the same realization."

Los Caballeros was a secret society dating back to our grandfather's grandfathers. Actually, generations beyond that, in Spain. When my ancestors and those of Press and the other members had immigrated to America, it continued on, meeting in the wine caves on the property of the same name since 1769.

Our unspoken mandate was to help those in need, whether they asked us to or not, but to always remain anonymous. If our anonymity ended with me, I'd never forgive myself. Nor would my father or grandfather.

"Brix will talk to Onyx," said Press.

If anyone could get through to him, it was our de facto leader, Gabriel "Brix" Avila—Onyx's cousin.

"Did I hear my name?" the man himself asked, joining Press and me.

"Onyx is threatening Los Caballeros," Press told him.

Brix pulled out a third chair and sat with us. "I've already spoken with him."

"And?" I asked.

"He'll drop it, but he has conditions."

I knew better than to ask what they were until we were somewhere we could ensure we were not overheard. I stood. "I'm going to check on Jada."

Brix shook his head. "That's one of his conditions."

"What? Does he seriously think I'll stay away from her?"

"If you don't, he'll not only come after you; he won't stop until he's ruined every one of us."

3

Jada

The more my brain connected with my body, the less I wished it would. Why the fuck had I wanted to feel?

Numb was good. *Feeling* brought the nightmares back. *Alone* brought them back too. And it didn't matter if I was awake or asleep. If I closed my eyes, I saw Al Zaabi. When I opened them, he was still there—as if the imprint of the memory was burned on my retinas. I wanted to scrub it away.

I didn't remember much about my father and the days and weeks right after he died. What stuck with me from that time of my life was my mama lying in bed beside me.

"Find a happy place in your mind, mija," she'd say. "Try to set the sadness aside." She told me to look for something safe that would either make me forget, for a few minutes, that my daddy was gone or for a memory of him that made me happy instead of sad.

Why couldn't I think of anything now? If my mind drifted to my childhood or when I was a teenager, every memory involved Luisa. I'd spent more time with her than anyone else, including my family. In more recent years, I was either in class, studying, or with Zin.

The two people I was closest to had a direct link to Al Zaabi.

I stared at the walls, up at the ceiling, then at the floor. What I really needed was to get the fuck out of this room. There wasn't even a window to look out of.

My muscles tightened when I heard footsteps approaching in the hall, then saw the doorknob turn slowly.

"You're awake." Montano crossed the room and sat in the chair where Zin had been. When my brother was here earlier, his presence had felt soothing, comforting. Now he was giving off an entirely different vibe.

"What's wrong?" I turned to him and asked. While he raised his head quickly, I'd already followed his line of sight.

"Is that blood on your hands?" I hugged myself when a chill traveled from my head to my feet.

"Sorry, sis. I thought I'd washed it all off." His eyes met mine. He stood and sat on the edge of the bed. "Hey, it's okay. No big deal."

"What's it from?" I demanded.

"Little scuffle. Like I said, no big deal."

"With who?"

Montano eased from the bed back into the chair. "Drop it, Jada."

What had been a chill turned into a tremor. "No, I won't fucking drop it. *What happened?*"

"Zin and I had a disagreement," he responded so quietly I could barely hear him.

"Disagreements rarely draw blood, brother."

He leaned forward and rested his elbows on his knees but folded his wrists so I couldn't see his hands. "Zin was in the wrong place at the wrong time," he muttered.

While I agreed, I found myself defending him. "He saved me."

My brother raised his head, and his eyes bored into mine. "*I* would've saved you."

"How would the outcome have changed? Would you feel like a big man for being the one who pulled the trigger?"

Montano's eyes scrunched. "What did you say?"

"You heard me. What's the difference whether you killed him or Zin did?"

"I would've taken him alive."

"You can't know that. It's what you wanted. You couldn't have guaranteed it."

"What's with the two of you anyway?" he asked.

"He's Press' best friend. I'm Luisa's. Make sense he'd get involved since the others were."

My brother snarled.

"What?"

"The others. Fucking Los Caballeros. That's what."

I rested my head against the pillow and looked up at the ceiling. "Most say they don't exist."

"You know they do."

I shrugged and shook my head.

"I'll tell you this; they won't exist beyond today."

I turned in his direction. "What's that supposed to mean?"

"Either they disband, or I'll see to it they regret it."

"Jesus, Montano, because your pride was wounded?"

"It isn't my pride, Jada. It's that one of their members put himself in the middle of a rescue mission.

While it was a success and you're safe, it could've gone very differently."

"But it didn't." I was so tired. I didn't have the energy to continue this conversation. "When can I go home?"

"That's up to Bones."

"Where is he?"

"I think he returned to the hospital."

I groaned and leaned against the pillow. "When will he be back?"

"Probably not until tomorrow morning."

I sat up and cried out when the numbness in my chest chose that moment to go away. *"Fuck!"* I screeched, crossing my arms in front of me, afraid to touch myself as much as I wanted to rub the pain away.

Montano stood and stroked my hair. "Take deep breaths, sis. Manage the pain."

I glared up at him. "Fuck off."

He raised a brow but continued what he was doing.

The door burst open, and Zin rushed into the room. *"What happened?"*

"My God, what happened to you?" I asked rather than answer. His nose was packed with gauze, and both of his eyes looked as though they were black.

Montano took a step in his direction, shoulders squared, fists clenched. "I told you to stay away," he seethed.

"Wait a minute," I shouted over him. "Is that what you did? Is that why your hands have blood on them? What the fuck?"

"Yes, and I'd do it all over again."

"So would I," Zin countered.

I stuck my fingers in my ears, and when neither stopped shouting, I screamed. *"Get out! Both of you, leave. Right now."*

They looked at me, then at each other.

"Why did you scream a few minutes ago?" Zin asked, attempting to approach the bed, but Onyx stepped in front of him.

"My sister is none of your business."

Zin's eyes met mine, and in them, I saw his question. I slowly shook my head. His brow furrowed, and his shoulders slumped. He wanted me to confess our relationship to Montano, but I couldn't. I wasn't sure I could still have one with him.

"Okay, I'll go," he mumbled. "I'll be in the other room if you need anything."

"She won't. Go home."

"Montano," I admonished. "You need to leave too. I want to rest."

"I'll sit with you," my brother offered.

"I don't want you here."

"Then, I'll stay," said Zin.

I shook my head. "I don't want either of you here. I don't want anyone here."

"Jada, you shouldn't be alone."

I glared at my brother. "That isn't your decision. Now, get out!" I raised my hand to point to the door but flinched when the movement caused the skin on my chest to stretch. Both men rushed over to me, one on either side of the bed.

"I'll take it from here," said another voice, coming from the direction of the door.

Montano looked over his shoulder. "It's okay, Tryst. I've got this."

Tryst's upper lip tightened. "I was not asking for your permission, Onyx."

"If I go, he goes." My brother pointed at Zin.

"You'll both go."

Zin motioned for Onyx to go first. When my brother wouldn't budge, Zin walked out the door.

"Hi, Tryst," I said when he walked over to the bed, leaned down, and kissed my cheek. The man wasn't my uncle, although I'd always thought of him that way. My mother's sister had been married to his brother before he passed away.

"How bad is the pain?" he asked.

So bad I didn't know how to respond. He meant physical pain, though, not what was really torturing me. "I don't know, maybe a seven," I replied.

"I am sorry this happened to you, Jada."

While I had no doubt others, maybe even everyone, felt the way he did, he was the first to say the words. "Thank you."

"What can I do to help?"

"I honestly don't know."

"Are you able to rest?"

I looked at him with wide eyes and shook my head.

"Will you hold my hands?" Tryst put his on my lap, and I put my palms on them. "Make yourself comfortable but keep your eyes focused on mine."

I rested my head on the pillow, but my gaze stayed on him.

"I'll tell you a story."

"Okay," I whispered.

"I was on a walk in Mexico one day. I was young, younger than you are now, and I got lost." He smiled. "Since I was in the Army at the time, I couldn't admit to anyone that a survivalist got himself lost in the wilderness, so I kept going, hoping I would come to a trail or, better, a road."

"Or another person?"

Tryst smiled a second time. "While you may think you know the story, I'm going to share a few things I've never told anyone."

I drifted in and out of sleep, trying so hard to keep listening as he told me about the day he'd stumbled on the property that was now his ranch. It was the same day he'd met the woman who would become his wife. Like him, Rosa had been visiting Mexico. She with her family, him with the military.

I'd never visited the place he called *El Lugar de Curación,* but listening to his story, I felt like I had. I could hear the rush of water in the creek he and Rosa had walked beside, and I could feel the warm breeze on my face when he described how soothing it felt.

"We crested a hillside and gasped as our eyes took in the view of the entire El Palomar valley. I told my Rosa I'd build her a house on the very ground we stood. It was a promise I kept."

I drifted deeper into sleep, but then woke with a start.

"What did you see?" Tryst asked when I gripped his hands and my eyes bored into his.

"A coyote. It was approaching me."

He nodded and closed his eyes, as if in prayer. When he opened them, he smiled.

4

When we left Jada's room, Onyx went in one direction and I went in the opposite, relieved when he didn't turn around and follow me.

"What happened?" Press asked when I found him waiting in the main sitting room.

"My guess is the anesthetic Bones put on Jada's wounds is wearing off. She must've moved in such a way that the pain caused her to scream." I shook my head. "Not that Onyx gave her the chance to answer when I asked."

"You two are oil and water, my friend."

"Why can't he understand I just want to help her heal?"

Press raised a brow.

"What?"

"Is he aware of the nature of your relationship?"

"No. It isn't up to me to tell him. Jada and I agreed to keep it between us. If she wants her brother to know, she has to be the one to tell him."

"You told me."

"Exactly. You're not just my friend, Press. I trust you more than anyone outside of my parents."

"What will you do now?"

I motioned for him to follow me outside. Once there, we sat on the porch steps. "I don't want to leave until I've had a chance to speak with her again."

"Ah. Your plan, then, is to outwait her brother. Likely, he is doing the same."

I rested my elbows on my knees and looked down at the flagstone that made up the walkway leading from the gravel driveway to the porch steps. Thousands of insects—ants—scurried in and out of the sand surrounding the stone. If I stood and walked to my car, I'd likely squash hundreds of them. Hundreds of innocent ants going about their day, gathering food for their colony, oblivious to anything happening in the bigger world beyond them. Like human trafficking victims. Like Jada.

After two days and nights of mind-blowing sex, she got out of the shower we'd shared, grabbed a change of clothes from the stash she kept at my place, dressed, kissed me goodbye after downing a cup of coffee, and drove off. I knew I'd hear from her later. And if I didn't, I'd send her a text. It wasn't necessary for either of us to say it. It was a pattern we'd settled into over the course of the last four years.

Instead, she'd left my house and was intercepted somewhere between there and her place by a man who'd abducted and tortured her.

"Why her?" I said out loud, not meaning to.

Press, of all people, knew why. Al Zaabi wanted Luisa. Jada was taken in her place.

"Don't answer that." I glanced over at him.

Press' gaze was focused on the vineyards in front of us.

"Earlier, I told you I love Jada."

He nodded.

"You're the first person I've said that to. Not Jada. How fucked up is that? Worse, I didn't realize it myself until I saw her naked and tied to a wall."

"Sometimes it takes a significant, life-altering event for us to recognize what's been inside of us for some time."

"What if I had told her, Press? What if, instead of hiding our relationship, we'd come clean months ago?

What if instead of her leaving my house, she and I had gone out to breakfast? Or I'd gone home with her?"

He took a deep breath and let it out slowly. "There are infinite what-ifs, my friend. None will alter the chain of events."

"It doesn't stop me from wondering."

"Why did you keep what's between you a secret?"

I shrugged. "The first time we had sex was after a crush party. We were at Los Cab, in fact. I guess we both thought it was a onetime thing."

"How long ago was that?"

I knew he'd ask, as much as I didn't want to answer. "Four years." It wasn't as though we saw each other often. It became more so gradually. Even after all this time, we'd still go days, sometimes weeks, without hooking up.

When I arrived home the day before New Year's Eve and found Jada waiting for me, it was the first I'd seen her in two weeks. Actually, I'd seen her, but it was the first time I was alone with her. We'd argued prior to that. Over something so insignificant. I couldn't remember what it was.

"I just want her to be okay again. I want to help her get there."

Press studied me with scrunched eyes.

"What? Could you say you didn't want the same thing for Luisa? Shit, Press, you hired a counselor to come to your house, where you insisted she stay. You didn't even know her."

"Nothing is as simple as it seems."

I wanted to ask him to elaborate, but the front door opened behind us. I glanced over my shoulder and saw Onyx. Doc followed.

"I told you to leave."

"Onyx," Doc admonished. "Zin is a guest here."

"I don't want him near my sister."

Doc put his hand on the man's shoulder. "I'll handle things. You need to talk with your family."

Onyx turned and scowled at me before accepting Doc's embrace. "I'll be back later." He skirted around Press and me, then walked across the flagstone where I'd studied the insects earlier.

"They never saw it coming," I said, looking down at the dead ants he'd stepped on.

"What are you talking about?" Press asked.

"It happens every day. People are abducted, taken from their homes, their countries, maybe tortured, maybe forced into the sex trade or slave labor, or they're killed. Like the ants." I pointed to the flagstone.

"Some say as many as forty million at any given time," he muttered.

"And they never saw it coming," I repeated.

"Give it a few minutes, then you can talk to her," said Doc before going back inside.

I waited as Doc had suggested before returning to Jada's room. When I did, I eased the door open and saw Tryst seated beside the bed. His hands held hers, and it appeared she was sleeping peacefully.

As much as I wanted to talk to her, reassure her I was here if she needed me and if I left, I'd come back, I didn't want to wake her. So I raised my phone, and Tryst nodded.

After walking out and closing the door, I stood in the hallway and sent a text message, asking Tryst to pass a message on to Jada. I waited for his response saying he would.

Once I received it, I went back outside to where Press still sat. Luisa was with him.

"I'm going home," I told them. "Jada's resting, and Tryst is with her."

"We're staying here," said Press, motioning to one of the stone guest cottages that were only a few yards from the main house. Press had a place about thirty minutes west of Butler Ranch, but I was sure Luisa wouldn't want to be that far away from Jada. My house was less than five miles from here, and right now, that felt too far.

"Glad to hear it. If she asks for me, I'll come right back. Otherwise, I'll return later or in the morning."

"I'll walk you to your car," Press offered. "The same goes for you," he said when I reached to open the driver's door. "If you need anything at all, I'll come to you."

"Luisa needs you more than I do."

He shook his head. "Luisa's family is here, as are the Butlers and Tryst. You, my friend, will be alone."

We embraced. "Thanks, Press."

"Call your parents," he said after I'd climbed into the car. "They'll want to know."

It was good advice. There was so much I had to tell them. Not just about Jada, but about Onyx's threat to take down Los Caballeros. My father had been a member before me. He needed to prepare himself, depending on how far Yáñez decided to take things.

I waited until I was home and had poured a glass of Scotch before calling my dad. When it went to voice-mail, I hung up and sent a text, asking him to return my call when he had a minute.

I stuck the phone in my pocket, grabbed the bottle of booze, and went into the room that was just like any other living room to me, but that Jada called the study.

Everything in it reminded me of her. Then again, everywhere I looked, no matter what room it was, would.

How many times had I used my arm to brush off whatever sat on my desk so I could fuck Jada on its surface? How many times had she and I cuddled naked under a blanket in front of the fireplace I'd just lit?

I sat in one of two chairs that faced it, tossed back the golden-brown liquid in my glass, then poured another despite the burn of it sliding down my throat. Then I dug my phone out of my pocket and swiped the screen, realizing how often I did that, hoping there'd be a text from Jada.

There wasn't one, not that I expected there to be. I scrolled through the history anyway. The last I'd received from her was from over two weeks ago, before we argued about something I couldn't remember. Three words. *On my way.* I'd give anything to go back to that day.

I scrolled more, until I found a photo she'd sent. I'd asked what she was doing, and when she responded that she was in the bath, I'd told her to send me a picture. She had. From the neck up with a big, beautiful, sly smile on her face. I saved the image, then swiped over to the collection of photos I had of her.

Before going through them, I had two more shots of Scotch, hoping the effects of the liquor would hurry up and kick in. Given I hadn't eaten since last night, I doubted it would take too much longer.

There were photos she'd sent when we were apart, along with pictures I'd taken when we were together. One of my favorites was of her right as she'd woken up after a night spent in my bed. I doubted she knew I'd taken it. If she had, I'm sure she would've asked I delete it.

Her hair was wild, some of it plastered to her fore-head, where the sweat from our fucking had dried it. The sheet had slipped down enough for her pink nipple to peek over the edge of it, and even in her sleep, Jada smiled.

Jada always smiled. It was what had drawn me to her all those years ago, back when she was hands-off to me.

I'd known her most of my life. Or at least of her. She was Onyx's little sister. Back then, we called him Montano. Nine years separated Jada and me. She was sixteen the day I'd first noticed her smile, her big brown eyes, and her body that had changed from that of a little girl to one that had gone through puberty.

I was twenty-five and had just graduated from law school but was working at KCRP, SLO CAL's under-ground radio station, while I waited to take the bar.

That was how I knew where Al Zaabi had her. Doc had shown me the video he'd sent to demand Luisa surrender herself to him in exchange for Jada. All those years ago, I'd used several pieces of blue painter's tape to affix the cover back on the on-air sign. It had been a dead giveaway when I saw it in the background.

I hadn't told Doc I knew where it was. In the split second I went from wondering to knowing, I made the decision not to divulge it. Deep inside me, I knew if I told him, he'd never allow me to help rescue her.

Luisa had seen the video too, recognized the blue tape like I had, and alerted Doc and the K19 team as to Jada's whereabouts.

She and Jada were at the station the day I'd repaired the sign. The day I knew I wanted her but could never have her. She was way too young for me, in addition to being the youngest sister of a good friend.

I shook my head. If Onyx had known my thoughts back then, he would've broken my nose the same way he had today.

As I scrolled through more photos, most from the last few months, I studied Jada's face. Zooming in on her dimples, her eyes, her smile, I could hear her voice, her laugh, feel her warmth, her sense of humor, her fucking sexiness.

The woman lying in bed in the room at Butler Ranch was nothing like the one in these photos. It was more than how she looked. It was everything. Her aura had shifted. How long would it be until it shifted back?

It had been less than thirty-six hours since my cock was buried deep inside her pussy, and I longed for her like a starving man. How in the hell had I gone two weeks without seeing her, holding her? How would I manage if Onyx followed through with his threat? Would I be able to choose Los Caballeros—its history, its members, the good we did, what it meant to my family—over Jada?

My cell vibrated in my hand, jarring me out of my thoughts. I took another swig of Scotch and answered my father's call.

5

Jada

I raised my head when I heard the door open and looked over at Tryst, slumped in the chair by the bed, asleep.

"Hi," whispered Bones, walking over to me. "How are you feeling?"

"Okay." My voice cracked, and I tried to clear it. I put my hand on my neck and closed my eyes. "Fuck, that hurts."

He handed me a bottle that sat on the table beside the bed. "Use this as often as you need it. It'll help." After spraying my throat, I gave it back to him.

"Where am I?"

"Butler Ranch. Sorry, someone should've told you that earlier." He fussed with the leads attached to my arms. "I'm going to give you more pain meds," he said, raising my arm and looking at the IV site. "Hey, Tryst."

I turned my head and saw him stand and stretch.

"You don't have to stay. Go get some sleep."

He shook his head, bent at the waist, and touched his toes. The man was more flexible than I was, and he was at least twenty years older.

I knew the minute the medication entered my bloodstream; it felt warm and I became groggy.

"Tryst, I need to change Jada's dressings. I'm going to ask you to step out while I do."

He stood upright, and our eyes met.

"I'll be okay," I told him.

When Tryst left the room, Bones pulled the sheet down to my waist. "I'll also reapply the analgesic to give you some pain relief beyond what you're getting intravenously."

"When can I leave?"

When Bones didn't answer right away, I knew he was weighing his words. "I'll know more tomorrow." He held out his arm. "Grab a hold of me and sit up."

"What will you know tomorrow that you don't know now?" I asked as he helped me straighten.

"How you're managing your pain, among other things."

"You know I'm going to keep asking until you tell me. What else?"

"Your mental state. Where you'll go from here."

His words stunned me. Couldn't I just go home?

"Take several deep breaths for me." Bones untied the straps on the back of the gown I wore and eased it from my shoulders.

"Jesus fucking Christ," I hissed, looking down at the marks crossing my chest and abdomen after he'd removed the dressing. I closed my eyes and took the breaths Bones had told me to.

"I'm sorry, Jada," he said as he dabbed the cream onto my flesh.

I opened my eyes. "I'm going to be sick."

He stopped what he was doing, reached behind him, and held a plastic basin near my mouth. My arm was still wrapped in his, and when I tried to let go, he put his hand on mine. "Go ahead. Hold onto me."

I retched, but nothing came out besides saliva. "Fuck, that hurt," I repeated.

"Lean back for me," he said when I shook my head and he took the basin away. "Shut your eyes."

I could feel him dabbing my wounds, but between the IV meds and the cream he applied, the longer he did it, the less pain there was.

"Will I have to go to a hospital?" I asked.

"No, but you will need to go somewhere you're cared for. It'll be a few days, maybe longer, before you're able to navigate on your own. You'll need help changing your dressings and applying the cream at least."

"No way," I muttered. "No one is looking at that."

Bones pulled up the gown and refastened the straps in the back. He sat beside me on the bed. "Then, you'll need to stay here."

"I can apply the cream, Bones. I'll stand in front of a mirror."

"I'll be back in the morning. We'll talk more then. Do you want me to give you something to help you sleep?"

I wasn't sure I'd need it in addition to what he'd given me for the pain. However, since he asked, it probably meant I would.

"Sure," I answered.

"Sorcha has been asking if she can come in. She promised not to talk. She just wants to be here in case you wake up and need anything."

I'd known Sorcha—Doc Butler's mother—since I was a little girl. The woman was like a mama bear combined with a hurricane. I'd never known someone so energetic or fierce.

"She doesn't have to."

"I agree that, for the time being, you shouldn't be alone, Jada. What about Luisa? Would you be more comfortable if she was with you?"

I shook my head and watched him use a syringe to give me something else through the IV.

"Get some rest, kiddo, and I'll see you in the morning."

"When does the dressing need to be changed again?"

"Then," he responded.

"Can you do it?"

"Of course."

When he walked out, I pulled the sheet up to my neck. It was bad enough Bones had to see what Al Zaabi had done to me. I didn't want anyone else to.

When I heard footsteps, I closed my eyes and feigned sleep. I knew if she thought I was out, Sorcha would keep her promise not to speak. Right now, I didn't want to talk to anyone. I didn't want anyone close to me. All I wanted was to be invisible.

When I opened my eyes, I was alone. I checked the time and saw it was eight in the morning. I knew Sorcha had been with me for part of the night since I woke up and found her sitting in the chair by the bed. Maybe she'd taken a break or was getting rest herself.

I hadn't dreamed much last night. At least nothing I remembered. Whatever Bones had given me to help me sleep must've done the trick. I wondered if it had a daytime version. Something that would turn the bad thoughts off.

"Come in," I said when I heard a soft knock on the door.

"Good morning," said Tryst, walking over to the bed. He kissed my forehead, then sat in the chair. "How did you sleep?"

"Bones gave me something that knocked me out."

I studied him. There was a look on his face I didn't remember seeing yesterday. His eyes were soft, and his head was slightly cocked. He *pitied* me. *Jesus.*

"Don't," I whispered.

His expression didn't change. "Jada—"

"Don't fucking pity me, Tryst."

"You have suffered trauma. What you see is concern, not pity, little one."

I closed my eyes and rested my head against the pillow, wondering when Bones would return. When he did, I intended to ask him to pile on the pain meds and maybe give me more of the stuff that would make me sleep. If I could be out twenty-four hours a day, I would, but only if the medication kept the nightmares away.

My eyes sprung open when Al Zaabi reappeared as if I'd conjured him. His fucking sneer. The way he'd practice with the whip, then suddenly strike me with it. It was better when it happened that way. Each time he told me I deserved the punishment I was about to get, the anticipation of the lashes was almost as bad as when the leather connected with my flesh.

"What day is it?" I asked Tryst.

"Tuesday, the third of January."

Forty-eight hours ago, I left Zin's house, intending to go home. *Forty-eight hours.* It felt like a lifetime. How fucking stupid had I been, stopping when I saw a car pulled off the side of the road and a man waving for help? This was wine country, though. We were a community of friends and neighbors. I'd known everyone who lived here all my life. We stopped and helped when someone needed it, whether we recognized the person or not.

I hated that the actions of one man would change that. People—women especially—would be warned not to stop to help strangers. It would never be the way it was before; no matter how much time passed, people would live in fear. *It fucking sucked.*

When the door opened, I was relieved to see Bones walk in. "Good morning, Jada, Tryst."

"Shall I step out?" Tryst asked.

Bones nodded. "For a few minutes, please."

Tryst leaned down and kissed my forehead again before walking out of the room.

"How are you doing?"

"I was hoping you could knock me out again."

He raised a brow.

"Is it bad that I'd rather not be present in my own life?" I sighed. "Don't answer that." No doubt if he did, it would be to remind me I was lucky to be alive. Lucky I had a life to be present in.

This wasn't my life, though. Nothing like it. In the same way Al Zaabi had changed how people in our community would treat strangers, he'd fucking changed *me*.

Tears I didn't bother hiding flowed down my cheeks.

"I know this is difficult, Jada—"

"Difficult? The motherfucking *sonuvabitch* should've just killed me. He took my life from me."

I'd no sooner said the words than the door opened and Montano walked in with my mother.

"Oh, mija," she cried. "Oh my God."

I glared at my brother when my mother sat at my bedside and cried. Why didn't he ask me before bringing her here? Jesus. I wasn't ready for this.

"Mom, the doctor was about to change my dressing. Can you come back in a few minutes?"

She looked up at me with scrunched eyes, then at Bones. "Okay," she said, standing.

Montano led her from the room but looked over his shoulder before walking out. "Sorry, sis."

The door closed without him seeing I'd flipped him off. "That thing I said about knocking me out? I need you to do it now even more."

"This is for pain," he said, holding a syringe in his hand. "I'm also giving you antibiotics to stave off infection."

"Is that it?"

Bones' eyes met mine. "Rest is the best thing for you right now."

"Thank God," I said under my breath.

Like last night, he untied the straps of my gown and lowered it in the front. I kept my eyes closed while he removed the dressing and applied more of the cream. "I'm going to have one of the nurses I work with stop by this afternoon since I have surgery scheduled. Her name is Lynne Sanchez."

"Is it necessary?"

"We need to manage your pain, Jada."

"Just put me out, Bones." I didn't want a stranger showing up here. I didn't want to talk to my mother. I didn't want to talk to anyone. Why couldn't I just be left alone?

Seconds after Bones put the contents of the third syringe through the IV, blissful sleepiness spread throughout my body. "Thanks," I whispered before letting the blackness engulf me.

6

Zin

My conversation with my parents, the night before, shouldn't have surprised me. Out of the many things I'd learned from them, making sure I had my priorities straight was a big one.

When I was in law school, my dad forbade me from setting foot in the vineyards during crush. "Once you're here, you'll never leave," he'd said. "Your job now is to pass the bar, not to pick grapes."

While last night's conversation was entirely different, its gist was the same. My parents were sitting next to each other at the dining room table when I answered the video call.

They both gasped when they saw me. "What in God's name happened to you?" my mother asked.

"I'll explain in a minute. I have a lot to tell you both," I began. "First, I want you to know I've been seeing Jada Yáñez."

"Is she one of Montano's sisters?" my mom asked, her eyebrow raised, perhaps because I'd avoided answering why I looked like I was in a bar fight.

"She is. The youngest." I watched both for a reaction, given our age difference, but it didn't seem to faze them. "I have been for the last four years." The look on their faces I'd anticipated with my first statement appeared with my last one. My dad masked it quicker than my mother did.

"That's a long time," she muttered, glancing over at him.

"Listen, there's something more important I need to talk to you about. Several things, actually."

My mom became emotional when I told her about Jada's abduction, and my dad's face turned ashen. The next part was harder to confess. "I killed the guy who took her." My mother's hand flew to her mouth as I looked into my father's eyes. "He was going to kill her."

My dad put his arm around my mother, and I waited for them both to process what I'd said.

"I'm okay, Michael," she told him, wiping away her tears. "Thank God you're all right, Vaile. How is Jada?"

"She's—" my voice cracked. I couldn't think too much about Jada right now, or I'd never get through the rest of this conversation. "I'm sorry I'm not telling you this in person. Dad, there's more."

His eyes scrunched, and they bored into mine. I nodded once.

"Will you be okay on your own for a few minutes, Evelyn?" he said, turning to my mother. I had no doubt she was well aware of Los Caballeros. That didn't mean my father would feel comfortable talking about it in front of her.

"I'll get straight to the point," I said when my mom walked out of the room. "Onyx Yáñez is threatening Los Caballeros unless I stay away from Jada."

My dad folded his arms and leaned closer to the screen. "What's behind his threat?"

"I interfered with the op K19 had in place to rescue her. Which, by the way, is why he did this to my face."

My father was quiet for at least a couple of minutes. I knew better than to push him, though. Patience was another thing I'd learned from him and my mom.

"She's important to you." He phrased it as a statement, not a question.

"I love her."

"Los Caballeros will weather the storm, son."

"He's threatening the members individually, too."

"He won't get very far down that road."

"Dad, I'm not going to be able to—"

"Your priority is Jada, Vaile." I was stunned he'd interrupted me; however, not that he knew what I'd been about to say. Like me, my father was an attorney, but he had retired to work full time in the vineyards. Not that he had to work at all. Our family's net worth was in the billions.

What he said instead, though, surprised me. "I'd like to suggest you call an emergency meeting. I'll fly down from Napa for it and get some of the other guys to join us."

Before ending the call, I told him I'd let him know when I could make it happen as soon as I was able to reach Brix, and also that Tryst was already in town. I also asked him to tell my mom I loved her and to, please, explain to her why I looked the way I did.

The meeting was scheduled for this evening since Press' father, Martin Barrett, was flying in from London.

I checked the time; it was a little after nine in the morning, so I sent a message to Press, asking if he or Luisa had seen Jada yet today. He responded they hadn't.

Is Onyx there?

Negative.

Heading over.

When he responded with a thumbs-up, I was already on the way to my car.

I pulled up and was about to park near the main house when Doc came out the front door.

"Fuck," I muttered, anticipating he'd tell me to leave.

"Hey, Zin."

"Doc."

He held up a remote, and a garage door opened in the winery building. "Pull in there," he said, motioning to it. "Then follow me around back."

Given he hadn't ordered me off his family's property, I was happy to do as he asked.

"Jada's sleeping," he said when I joined him in the courtyard behind the main house. Emotion overtook me when he invited me to take a seat on a bench under the gazebo.

"This is the first place I kissed her," I confessed. "Actually, she kissed me."

Doc chuckled. "That doesn't surprise me. Jada's always reminded me of her cousin and my sister-in-law, Alex."

"They even look alike," I said, nodding.

"Biggest ballbusters in the valley, but also two of the best people I know."

I agreed.

"We might not have a lot of time, so I'll get straight to the point."

"Go ahead."

"The Butler family has enjoyed a symbiotic relationship with the members of Los Caballeros for many years. So much so that my father has volunteered to step in on your behalf."

I was about to speak, but he held up his hand. "He and I will be attending your meeting at the caves tonight."

While we'd met at Press' place on the coast in Cambria with outsiders in attendance, no one—and by that, I meant absolutely no one—outside the members had ever attended a meeting at the caves.

Doc's father, Laird "Burns" Butler, was a legend, though. Not just within the wine industry, but also in the intelligence world. According to what I'd heard, he was a spyware mastermind.

"You may or may not know Onyx works for me. He runs one of my company's newer teams, and I respect the hell out of him. I'd rather not play the boss card if I can help it. I'd like him to back down on his own."

"But you don't think he will."

"Onyx is as stubborn as they come, so I'd prefer we develop antidotal measures if he proceeds with his threat."

"Understood." I looked down at the ground. "I can't stay away from Jada. I won't."

Doc shook his head. "If I thought you should, we wouldn't be having this conversation." He looked over at me. "Where's the stuff I gave you for your nose?"

"I couldn't breathe with it in."

He took a closer look. "Has it bled today?"

"Not a drop."

"You're lucky. It might not be as bad as I thought." He turned his head. "Back to what we were talking about; I had a conversation with Tryst, and he's worried

Jada is withdrawing. He's going to suggest she stay with him at his ranch."

"It's a good idea."

"Here's the stipulation, Zin. He's asking you not to join them in Mexico until he invites you."

"What does that mean?"

"I'm not certain."

"So much for you not thinking I should stay away from her."

His eyes met mine. "We all want what's best for Jada. If Tryst believes it will help her if you're with them at the ranch, he'll say so. In the meantime, we're going to get Onyx off your back."

"Can I see her now?"

"Head on in. Merrigan came up with a reason she needed to meet with Onyx this morning. You have about an hour before she'll be back. I wouldn't be surprised if he came with her."

I thanked him and went inside.

"Oh dear. Look at you," said Sorcha in her thick Scottish brogue.

"I'd tell you it looks worse than it feels, but I'd be lying."

She shook her head and refocused her attention on what she was cooking. I took it as a sign to leave.

"Wait," she said as I was walking away. "You should know Jada called out for you in her sleep last night."

"She did?"

"Several times, in fact. I stayed with her until dawn."

"Nightmares?"

"Perhaps so, but she was asking for you."

"Thanks for telling me, Sorcha. I wasn't sure she'd want to see me."

She smirked and winked. "She doesn't, but her subconscious is on your side."

I thanked her again, anxious to get to Jada before Onyx returned with Merrigan.

I knocked softly and eased the door open when I didn't hear a response. Tryst was sitting in the chair beside the bed and put his finger in front of his lips.

When he stood, I followed him into the hallway.

"Bones gave her something to help her sleep," he explained.

"Doc mentioned you think it would be a good idea for her to visit your ranch."

Tryst nodded once.

"He also told me I needed to wait for an invitation to go myself."

He walked farther down the hall, and I followed. "I have not yet broached the subject with Jada. She may not want to go. If she does and she wants you to accompany her, then by all means, you should."

"You don't think she will, though."

He nodded a second time. "She's withdrawing."

"Doc mentioned you said the same thing to him."

Tryst motioned to her door. "Go ahead, now. I'll stand watch."

I smiled, thanked him, and returned to Jada's room. When I eased through the door, her eyes were open. I walked closer to the bed, wishing I could touch her, kiss her, have some kind of physical contact, but after her reaction yesterday, I held back.

"You shouldn't be here."

"I won't stay long. I just wanted to see you, make sure you were okay."

She turned her head, and her eyes met mine. "I'm not, Zin. I might never be."

I sat in the chair. "Don't say that. You'll heal, and little by little, you'll feel like your old self again."

She opened her mouth as if to speak, but shut it.

"What were you going to say?"

She rested her head against the pillow. "I won't ever be my 'old self' again, Zin. Al Zaabi took that away from me."

"I'm sure with counseling—"

She shook her head. "Don't."

"I'm sorry. I'm just…trying, you know?"

"Stop. There's no reason for you to."

"No reason to try? Jada, I…" As much as I wanted to tell her I loved her, now didn't feel like the right time. She'd think I was only saying it because of what had happened to her.

"You should go."

I stood, leaned over, and kissed her forehead. I couldn't help myself. "I'll be back."

"Goodbye, Zin."

In four years, she'd never once said goodbye to me. It was always, "See ya," or "Later." I tried not to read too much into it, hoping she didn't mean it.

7

Jada

There was a parade of people who came to my room to keep me company throughout the afternoon and evening. Thankfully, the medication Bones gave me made me sleepy enough that no one stayed long.

After Zin left, I dozed off and on, wishing that when I woke, he'd be back. At the same time, I was relieved he wasn't. The sooner Zin and I realized we had no future, the better.

For him, it meant getting my brother to let go of his anger and forgive him without carrying through with his threat to ruin him.

For me, it meant I'd get my wish to be left alone.

It was only when I began feeling sorry for myself that I'd cry. It was pointless, though. It wasn't like I could go back and change the events of the last few days.

I wasn't the same person I had been when I woke up on New Year's Day. The outside of my body had been irrevocably changed, but not to the extent the inside had.

I was plagued by nightmares, awake and asleep, that I knew would never go away. How could my brain turn off the memories of what had happened to me? How many people lived through the type of trauma I had and truly recovered from it?

As far as the marks Al Zaabi had left on my body, I could barely look at them myself without feeling nauseated. They covered my chest, crisscrossing my breasts down into my torso.

Zin would certainly never look at my body the way he had before.

"God, you're perfect," I could hear him say as he knelt before me, his lips trailing over every inch of my nakedness. Not anymore. Now, I wasn't even desirable. I was damaged.

It wouldn't just be men who found me repulsive. Once women saw the scars I had, no doubt they'd be horrified too. And what about children? I'd be a freak show.

As for other men, I'd known from the first time Zin noticed me, when I was still a teenager, that no other would do it for me the way he did. Five years passed before he and I had sex for the first time. By then, I was twenty-one and Zin was thirty.

I'd been with other guys, and I knew Zin had had plenty of women in his life, none he was serious about, according to him. After that first time, though, neither of us had sex with anyone else.

Early on, it was because I had no interest in being with another man. While that remained the case, several months in, Zin had specifically brought it up when we were lying in bed one night.

"I don't want you seeing other men," he'd said.

I'd gotten out of bed, then stunned him by climbing on top of him and straddling his torso. "I don't want you seeing other women."

"I haven't."

"Neither have I."

It was the one and only time we'd talked about it. Periodically, we'd talk about whether we wanted to go public with our relationship. It wasn't that either of us had said we wanted to continue keeping it a secret; it just turned out that way. After we passed the two-year mark, it became more about our friends and family giving us shit for not telling them sooner.

We also didn't spend that much time together. I was in law school, and he had a thriving law practice. It kept him as busy as I was, without counting the time he spent with his friends.

I wondered, once they found out, if people would think I wanted to be a lawyer because of him. That wasn't the reason. In fact, I'd decided that was what I wanted to be long before I knew him as more than my older brother's friend.

It was Luisa and what had happened to her and her family that led me to the decision. When we were in middle school, her father drove drunk and got into an accident, killing a family of four. While I didn't condone what he'd done, I saw Luisa's family lose everything as lawyers battled over whether the surviving members of the family killed should essentially take everything the Reeves owned. In the end, it was the two lawyers who took it all.

I'd vowed then not to let that happen to another family if I could help it. I didn't care if I had to work for free for most of my life. No one should lose their home and everything else they owned while lawyers lined their pockets.

It was something Zin and I had argued about often while I was still in law school. "After all the hard work and money it took for you to become an attorney, you don't think you're worth people paying for your expertise?" was what he'd most often said. Him, who could've worked for free all his life and still be a millionaire. Maybe even a billionaire. It made me sick.

While I graduated with my JD, I hadn't taken the bar yet. Now, I doubted I ever would. Becoming a lawyer meant planning a future, something I had no interest in doing anymore.

The nurse Bones said would stop by to check on me had just left after changing my dressing for the final time that night, when my brother walked in.

"Hey, sis," he said, attempting to sound like his usual jovial self, but looking at him, it was evident he was a wreck.

"What's going on, bro?"

Montano took a seat but didn't answer. After studying him for several minutes, my eyes drifted closed. When I opened them again, he was gone.

The following morning, Bones and Tryst arrived at the same time. However, Bones didn't ask him to step out. Instead, they each took a seat in one of the two chairs in the room.

"What's going on, guys?" I asked.

"I think you're doing well enough for me to remove the IV today. Your wounds are also healing more rapidly than I anticipated."

I looked between the two men with a raised brow.

"We want to talk to you about where you'll go from here."

"Home?" I tried to muster enough false enthusiasm to convince them I was happy about the possibility, but I doubted I was successful.

Given every cent I'd made went to law school tuition, I still hadn't moved out of my mother's house.

She'd come to visit twice more, along with two or three different siblings of mine each time. Neither visit went well. We barely spoke. She, my sisters, and even my brothers had cried. My mom had looked up at the ceiling—maybe she was talking to God—and repeatedly asked why this had happened to me. It was a question I'd asked myself countless times, and her doing so didn't help.

"Stop saying that!" I'd finally shouted. "It happened, okay? I'm sorry your darling baby girl isn't sweet and innocent anymore." I'd burst into tears and told her to leave. After several minutes, she did. That was late yesterday afternoon. I had no doubt she'd return sometime this morning.

"There are options for you to consider," said Bones. "First, Onyx said you can stay with him and Blanca at their place."

On the other side of the country? In the mountains, during winter? Staying with just the two of them in the tiny lakefront cabin they'd winterized in order to live there year-round didn't appeal to me at all. I shook my head.

"Sorcha and Laird have invited you to stay on here for as long as you'd like. Two of the three guest cottages are empty, so you could have your pick."

"I don't want to impose on them more than I already have."

"You should come stay with me at my ranch," said Tryst.

Of the four choices, it was the only one that interested me. "Are you sure?"

"I want you to, Jada."

"I would like to suggest you either establish care in Alamos or consider having a medical professional travel with you," said Bones.

"I wouldn't know where to start." Besides, the idea of having yet another stranger examine me, look at the marks on my chest and abdomen, was enough to nauseate me.

"Lynne said she'd be willing to go."

"I wouldn't be able to afford it."

"It won't be for long. Maybe just a few days, and I'm sure we could get insurance to pay for it," Bones suggested.

I doubted that very much and guessed either one of the men in the room intended to cover the cost, or maybe Zin had offered. However, even if I argued the point, I knew neither Tryst nor Bones would relent.

"When would we go?" I asked.

"We can leave whenever you'd like," Tryst responded.

"Tomorrow?"

He nodded. "Or this afternoon."

"That soon?"

"You can, or you can wait. Whichever you'd prefer," said Bones.

"Can I talk to Tryst alone for a minute?"

"Of course." Bones stood and walked out.

"Are you sure about this?" I asked.

"There is no better place for you than at *El Lugar de Curación*. It is the healing place." I'd heard before it was the direct translation of the name he'd given the ranch.

"I won't be imposing?"

Tryst leaned forward. "While you are not my niece by blood, you called me uncle until you decided you were too old to do so. I think you were thirteen."

I smiled. "That's about right."

"You are family, Jada, and family doesn't impose."

I bit my lip. "I don't want to go home, Tryst."

"I understand."

"I also don't want my mother to come with us. At least not right away. Actually, I don't want anyone to come."

"What about the nurse?" he asked.

I sighed, knowing if she traveled with us, Tryst would have less worry about my care. "The nurse should come, as long as she's still willing."

"I will respect your wishes to the letter."

"You're sure?"

Tryst smiled. "I'll make the travel arrangements."

After he left, I glanced over at the cell phone I hadn't used once on the bedside table. I didn't know who had found it or where. Maybe it had been in my car.

My car! What had happened to it? Was it still sitting on the side of the road where I'd stopped? I grabbed the phone, happy to see it was charged, and called my brother.

"Hey, sis," he answered on the first ring.

"Montano, do you know where my car is?"

"I took care of it. It's here at the house."

"Oh, um, good. I wondered. So, um, I'm leaving for Tryst's ranch today." I hoped my decision not to go to New York with him and his wife wouldn't hurt his feelings.

"I heard, and I think it's the right choice."

I breathed a sigh of relief. "I'm glad. I appreciate—"

"Say no more. By the way, we were just leaving to come over there."

"Who's we?"

"Everybody."

"Not the kids?" I had six brothers and two sisters. Montano, me, and Angelina, who was only a couple of years older than me, were the only ones without children. The rest had at least two each.

"No kids. They're in school or at the babysitter's. Just grown-ups."

"Spouses?"

"No spouses either."

"Thanks, Montano."

A little over two years ago, my brother had been in a plane crash and was in a coma for a month. When he came out of it, he'd had to learn to walk and talk again. While his recovery went faster than anyone anticipated, he'd hated every minute of it. He felt weak, he'd told me, and the fewer people visiting him while in rehab, the happier he was. I understood better now and was appreciative he knew I'd feel the same way.

When the call with my brother ended, I texted Luisa and asked if she and Press could come over to the main house. Five minutes later, they walked in.

After I told her I was going to Tryst's ranch, we hugged and I thanked her and Press for all they'd done for me.

Shortly after, my family came to see me. I waved when Press and Luisa walked out, saying I hoped to see them again before I left.

"I brought a suitcase," said Angelina, biting her lip and blinking away tears.

"You can cry if you need to," I told her.

"I'll wait."

I smiled through my own tears. "Always so strong, Angel."

She shook her head. "You're the strong one, Jada. You always have been."

Maybe that had been true at one point in my life, but no longer.

My family stayed for over an hour, made bearable only by the knowledge I'd soon be leaving the country and I wouldn't see them for several days. Maybe weeks. Or longer.

Bones removed the IV, and I dressed and waited in the main living room for Tryst to return. Doc and Merrigan joined me to say goodbye.

I also thanked Sorcha and Laird for allowing me to stay. I would've thanked their son and daughter-in-law who actually lived in the main house, but Sorcha said they were on holiday and had been since I arrived.

When Tryst returned, Press, his father, and Luisa followed him in the door.

"These two have offered us the use of their plane," said Tryst, pointing to father and son.

I wanted to tell them it wasn't necessary, but I had no idea how we'd get there otherwise.

"Would you mind if I ride along?" Luisa asked. "We won't stay very long."

"I'd love it."

A few minutes later, the five of us, along with my nurse, climbed into a waiting SUV and left Butler Ranch.

Zin lived on the same road—Adelaide Trail—and when we passed his house and I saw his car parked in the circular drive, my heart sank.

I couldn't believe he hadn't come to say goodbye, even though I was the one who'd repeatedly asked him to leave when he visited.

Luisa gripped my hand, and our eyes met.

"It's for the best," I whispered. It was time the thing between Zin and me ended, and while it made me sad, I knew it was, as I'd said, for the best.

8

Zin

"What do you mean she's gone?" I shouted into the phone when Bones picked up and told me Jada was no longer at Butler Ranch. "Where is she?"

"On her way to Mexico with Tryst."

"And nobody thought to tell me? Fuck."

"Sorry, Zin. I, uh, didn't realize you'd want to know."

"Thanks, Bones," I said, ending the call. I immediately contacted Press, but his phone went straight to voicemail.

I walked over to the almost-empty bottle of Scotch and poured the last of it into the glass just as my mom walked into the kitchen. She and my dad had stayed at my place after the meeting ended last night, rather than fly back to Napa since it was so late.

"Hey," I said, downing the golden-brown liquid.

She walked over and embraced me. "Little early in the day to break out the booze," she said, squeezing me.

"Jada left."

"Left?"

"She's on her way to Tryst Avila's ranch in Mexico." I opened the refrigerator, pulled out a beer, and popped it open. "She didn't say goodbye or, you know, thanks for saving my life." I took a swig and kept going until I'd drunk half the can.

My mother took it from my hand, set it on the counter, and led me over to the table in the breakfast nook. "Sit down and start talking. Go back to the beginning."

"I'd rather not, Mom."

"I didn't ask if you wanted to."

"You know I'm in my mid thirties, right?"

"You're not. There's no way I'm old enough to have a child that age."

"Either way, I think the days of you forcing me to tell you stuff I don't want to talk about are over."

She shook her head. "It doesn't work that way. Mothers reserve that right until they breathe their last breath."

"Jeez, don't say shit like that."

"Enough avoidance, Vaile. Start talking."

"I knew her. I mean, she was Montano's baby sister. That's how I thought of her. Not that I *thought* of her."

"Glad to hear it. Go on."

I told her about how Jada and Luisa had done an internship through their high school at the SLO CAL radio station, leaving out the part about that being the place where she was held captive. "I think she was sixteen at the time."

"And you were twenty-five."

"Nothing happened. I barely even talked to them. *Jeez.* Do you want me to tell you the story or not?"

She nodded and motioned with her hands for me to continue.

"Two years later, we were at an after-crush party at Butler Ranch. She'd just graduated from high school, and we talked. One thing led to another—"

My mother held up her hand. "I get the picture. You can skip this part."

"And we kissed. Once. That was it."

She raised a brow.

I shook my head. "Why would I lie?"

"Good point. How long before you saw her again?"

"I saw her around, but not enough to talk to. Three years later, after yet another crush party, things changed between us."

She counted on her fingers. "Four years ago, and you've been seeing each other since."

"Yeah, I mean, on and off."

"You've been sleeping with her."

"I thought you wanted to skip that part."

"I hope you used protection."

"That's it." I pushed my chair from the table, walked to the fridge, and grabbed another beer.

"I'll take one of those," she said, holding out her hand.

"What's this?" my dad asked, joining us.

"Jada left for Tryst's ranch and didn't say goodbye," my mom told him. "After having sex with him for the last four years."

I wanted to smash the beer can against my forehead. "Are you serious right now?"

My father walked over, leaned down, and kissed my mother's cheek. "I love it when you start drinking midafternoon."

"You do not. You always say I fall asleep before dinner."

"Speaking of dinner. I'm in the mood for oysters." My dad rubbed his stomach.

"I thought you were going back to Napa today."

"Given the circumstances, I think we should stay a couple more days. Don't you?"

I didn't. If they weren't leaving, it meant I couldn't pull out another bottle of Scotch and drown myself in it tonight.

"Didn't you two used to date?" my mother asked, pointing at the woman standing at the check-in desk when we arrived at my parents' favorite restaurant in Cambria. It was on Moonstone Beach Drive and had the best fresh seafood I'd ever had.

"We went out on one or two."

"I heard she owns this place now," said my dad.

"Is she single?"

I huffed and walked over to the woman we were discussing. "Hey, Stormy." We cheek-kissed.

"Zin, good to see you. And your parents," she added when they approached. "I have the front corner table open."

"Darn it. She's wearing a ring." My mother snapped her fingers after Stormy showed us to our seats, then walked away.

"Evelyn," my father said with a raised brow.

The inappropriateness of her comments must've dawned on her. My mother's cheeks turned pink. "Forgive me, Vaile. I was being insensitive."

"Look, I know it kind of seems like things are over between Jada and me, but it's going to take me some time to accept it."

"Sorry," she repeated.

"All I want to do is help, ya know?"

Both my mom and dad cocked their heads, studying me in the same way they had when I was growing up and we were having a conversation I'd later be mortified we'd had.

"Is it so wrong that I want to help her heal? Help her get back to normal?"

My mom sat back in her chair when my dad leaned forward. "She's not a project for you to take on, son."

"I know that."

"Do you?" he asked.

I scowled and took a drink of the wine my parents had ordered. No, I didn't see her as a fucking project. I just wanted to help. Why couldn't anyone understand that? It was a simple premise, and one that made sense, given I'd killed Al Zaabi to save her life. "I don't want to continue this conversation."

We ordered, shared a second bottle of wine, had dinner, and were on our way home without another word being said about Jada—thankfully.

I was glad my father was driving and my mom was in the front passenger seat when my cell vibrated. I pulled it out and saw a message from Press.

Just returned from taking Jada and Tryst to Mexico.

I felt as though I'd been punched again, this time in the gut and by Press rather than Onyx. What the fuck? He flew her there and didn't say a word to me? I threw the phone on the seat and stared out the window.

Maybe he'd thought it was best not to tell me after the dressing down I got at the meeting the night before. I'd come close to resigning from Los Caballeros. I still wondered if not doing so was the right decision, even though everyone had agreed the important thing was that Jada was alive.

However, no one thought I'd done the right thing by interfering, especially not Doc.

I stood by every decision I'd made, though, and if I had to do it over again, I wouldn't change a thing. I wouldn't even have tried to keep Al Zaabi alive. All that mattered was Jada.

"If you're looking for my resignation, you've got it," I'd said.

All heads turned in my direction.

Press was the first to speak. "No. Absolutely not."

"Agreed," said Ridge. "If Zin resigns, so do I."

"No one is resigning," said Brix. He looked down at Tryst, who was leading the meeting. "Sorry. Go ahead."

Tryst's eyes met mine. "As Brix said, no one is resigning. However, your actions could have had serious consequences. They still might if Onyx Yáñez remains determined we disband."

"We've faced worse," said Martin, glancing over his shoulder at Press. "Long before you and your brother were old enough to know what was going on."

I had no idea what he was talking about. However, the gentlemen seated at the table appeared to know.

"Are you going to enlighten us?" Ridge asked.

Tryst shook his head. "That is not the reason we are here tonight." He looked over at Burns.

"Yáñez has no evidence against Los Caballeros or any of its members," the elder Butler said without looking up.

"Are you certain?" Tryst asked.

"Yes," Doc answered for him.

"What about Al Zaabi?" I asked.

"Taken care of," Doc responded. "However, my recommendation is that Los Caballeros enter an extended period of inactivity." He, like Tryst, looked directly at me.

I wondered, now, if that was the reason Press hadn't said anything to me about Jada leaving. Did Doc's comment mean I was supposed to be frozen out?

First, he'd said he didn't think I should stay away from her, then he said he thought I should? What the fuck?

My eyes met my dad's in the rearview mirror, and I hated wondering if he was in on something I'd been left out of.

Once we'd returned to the house, I stayed outside when my parents went in.

"Hey, asshole," I said when Press answered my call.

"I take it no one told you she was leaving."

"That's right. Not even my best fucking friend."

"My apologies. I mean that sincerely."

"Too little, too late. Jada's gone, and I didn't get to see her before she left. As I'm sure you're aware, I'm also not welcome at the ranch until Tryst says so."

"If it makes you feel any better. She didn't want anyone to accompany her. Except Tryst, of course."

"I'm not *anyone*," I said before abruptly ending the call. I'd saved her fucking life. More, I loved her.

I sat on the grass, lay back, and looked up at the stars—one of Jada's favorite things to do. Whenever we did, it usually ended with both of us naked, fucking our brains out on the open lawn. Not that anyone would've been able to see us. This part of the property was surrounded by twelve hundred acres of some of the most valuable vineyards on the Central Coast. If someone as much as set foot on it, my phone would blow up with security alerts.

Damn, I missed her. But why? Why hadn't I felt this profound sense of loss two weeks ago? Why was I able to go days without missing her then, and now, hours away from her were making me crazy? Especially since I had no idea how long it would be before I'd be *permitted* to see her again.

How fucked up was that? I was about to get up and go inside when I saw a star shoot across the sky. Jada saw them all the time; I never did.

"You're not paying attention, Zin," she'd tell me.

Goddammit. Why hadn't I paid attention when it mattered? Why hadn't I paid more attention to *her*? Why hadn't I realized how much she meant to me *before* I lost her?

I kept staring at the sky, wishing another star would shoot across it. If it did, I'd make a wish. I'd forgotten to do that with the first one.

9

Jada

Pain from the wounds intensified once I left the bed and was in the SUV on the way to the airfield. Lynne, the nurse, had oral meds for me to take, but they didn't have the same immediate effect as the ones I'd received through the IV.

"How are you managing?" she asked from the third-row bench seat, where she sat with Tryst.

"Six."

She checked her watch. "Let me know if it worsens by the time we reach the plane."

I rested my head against the seat and closed my eyes. The first image that popped into my head was Zin's car parked in front of his house.

I turned toward the window so Luisa couldn't see when a tear ran down my cheek. I felt Tryst's hand rest on my shoulder. It was warm and reassuring. When others touched me, I flinched. Comfort from him was so much easier to accept than it was from anyone else.

It was the reason the decision to go to his ranch had been so easy to make.

Luisa's hand still rested on mine from a few minutes ago, and it was all I could do not to wrench it away. Instead, I eased it out from under hers and weaved my fingers on my lap.

When I heard her quick intake of breath, I turned my head to look at her. "I'm sorry," I whispered when I saw her brush away tears.

"Please don't be. I only wish there was more I could do."

"You have your own trauma to work through."

She shrugged. "Press has helped me so much. I don't know how I would've managed without him." She shook her head, and her gaze rested on the man who sat in the driver's seat. Her voice was so soft but so full of love that I hoped Press could hear her.

Her words made me think again about how easy it was for me to accept Tryst's help.

The trauma Luisa and I had suffered was so different. She'd woken up bound and gagged inside a shipping container where she spent days living in terror of what was happening and what would happen once the ship arrived at its destination.

Thank God, when the door had opened once the vessel docked, she and the others in the container with her were rescued. I'd asked if anyone had "hurt" her. At the time and again now, the word felt so small and inadequate to encompass the possible ways in which she may have been abused. However, she'd assured me she wasn't sexually assaulted, nor did it appear she'd been beaten.

I groaned inwardly. *She'd* assured *me*. I'd been no comfort to her at all. How fucked up was that?

"It's what everyone wants, Jada. Just to help you. I know Zin—"

"Don't," I snapped.

Luisa's mouth pursed, and she looked out the window.

"I'm sorry. I just…"

"It's okay," she whispered. "I actually know how you feel, so I shouldn't have pushed. I hated it when people did that to me."

It pissed me off that she'd bring up Zin, but as much as I wanted to reassure her it was "okay," like always, I couldn't. Had I always been like this? Had everything always been about me?

I closed my eyes, wishing I could just sleep. Not just now. The truth was, I never wanted to be awake again. At the speed at which Press was driving, if I opened the door and jumped out, I'd get my wish. I grabbed the handle, fingers twitching, and my eyes met his in the rearview mirror. Could he see where my hand rested, or did he just sense how on edge I was?

I let go, knowing that if I did decide I couldn't go on, it wouldn't be fair to end my life in the presence of so many people who cared about me—Luisa especially.

We arrived at Tryst's ranch after nightfall, but even by the light of the moon alone, I could see its beauty. More, a sense of calm settled over me, reinforcing that I'd made the right decision by coming here.

Tryst invited Luisa, Press, and his father to stay the night, but they insisted they wanted to return to the Central Coast.

After we thanked them and said goodbye, Tryst invited Lynne and me inside. "I think it would be best if the two of you stayed in the main house for the time being."

While I'd heard there were more *casitas* on the ranch, it hadn't occurred to me I'd stay in one of them. Thankfully, Tryst hadn't made that suggestion.

He showed us to our adjacent rooms, each with its own en suite bathroom. "I'm sure you're very tired." When I nodded, he kissed my forehead.

"Can I help you get settled?" Lynne asked after Tryst left us on our own.

"I'd like to wait until tomorrow."

"Of course. We don't need to change your dressing again tonight since we did it right before we left. However, it is time for more pain medication as well as something to help you sleep if you want it."

"Yes. Please," I said, thanking God, particularly when I saw her open a small cooler and remove a syringe.

"Do I need another IV?" I asked.

"Not unless you have a setback. I can give these to you via intramuscular injection, or IM."

I walked into the bathroom, resting my hands on the counter when dizziness overtook me and tears of frustration ran down my cheeks.

"Jada?"

"What?" I snapped.

"The fatigue you're experiencing is normal."

I bit the inside of my cheek to stop myself from telling her to fuck off and leave me alone. While that's what I wanted, first I needed her to give me the injection.

"Can I shower tomorrow?" I asked instead.

She stood in the doorway. "You can tonight if you'd like."

"Too tired. I would like to brush my teeth, though."

As difficult as it was for me to accept help, when just raising my arm felt insurmountable, I relented and let her get my toothbrush and paste ready, then hand it to me.

"I know this is difficult for you, Jada, and believe me, the last thing I want to do is make you uncomfortable. Part of being a healthcare provider means learning how not to take things personally. You can tell me to leave you alone, even to fuck off, and it won't change anything as far as I'm concerned."

I smiled. I actually fucking smiled. "Really?" I said after spitting in the sink. "I can tell you to fuck off?"

Lynne nodded. "Hourly, if it makes you feel better."

"I just might take you up on it," I said, letting her help me change clothes and get in bed far less reluctantly than I might have.

When I woke the next morning after another night without remembering dreaming, I saw a robe hanging on a hook on the back of the door. I got out of bed, put it on, then managed to brush my teeth on my own before walking out of the bedroom and following the sound of conversation.

"Good morning, little one," said Tryst. "Coffee?"

"Bless you," I said, taking a seat at the table, where Lynne also sat.

"How's your pain this morning?" she asked.

"Um, four maybe? My pain receptors are probably still asleep."

She smiled. "That would be a good thing. It would mean we still have time to get ahead of it." She stood and left the room.

"She's nice," I said to Tryst when he set a cup in front of me along with cream and sugar, then sat beside me after pouring his own cup. "I just realized you used to call me little one when I was a child. I'd forgotten."

"You were very small."

"Onyx used to call me the runt."

"Your birth was difficult."

I took a sip of my coffee. "It was? No one's ever told me that."

Tryst nodded. "Your mother came close to dying in childbirth."

I set the coffee on the table hard enough for the hot liquid to splash on my hand. "Are you serious? Why wouldn't she tell me that?"

He shrugged. "Perhaps because it was not your fault."

His words stunned me, given I was falling down that very rabbit hole. "If you think about it, it was. She wouldn't have almost died if she weren't pregnant with me."

"You have your answer. Your mother knew you would feel responsible."

I'd never thought of my mother as a selfless person, particularly given her behavior over the last couple of days. But maybe I'd been unfair to her.

"Tryst?"

He raised his head. "Yes?"

"Am I a selfish person?"

"Selfish? No. I wouldn't say so."

My eyes teared up at his response. "What would you say?"

He crossed his arms, rested them on the table, and leaned forward. "Why are you asking?"

I looked over my shoulder when Lynne returned. "Oral or IM?" she asked.

"I'm supposed to say oral, right?"

She shook her head. "You'll eventually transition away from IM, but don't be too tough on yourself now when it isn't necessary."

"IM please."

After giving me the shot, she excused herself.

"I will say the same thing to you, Jada. Do not be too tough on yourself right now."

I told him about my reaction when Luisa returned from the UK and how I felt like a shitty friend. "What you said about my mom…I wonder how far off I am in how I see people. Including myself."

"When you're ready, we'll visit the meditation center. It will be a good place for you to think about such things."

"Ready today or ready another time?"

He smiled. "When you're ready."

After breakfast, Lynne helped me shower by wrapping my wounds. Afterward, she changed my dressing, then suggested I take a nap.

When I woke screaming, Tryst was standing beside me, his brow furrowed.

"Al Zaabi," I whispered. The dream had changed. This time, instead of him raising his whip or screaming at me, I could see his eyes at the exact moment Zin's bullet had penetrated his body. Instead of black, as I remembered them, they glowed red, as if he were the devil. "You will pay," he seethed right before I woke up. In reality, he'd died instantly, a split second before he intended to kill me. He hadn't spoken, and his eyes were closed.

Tryst sat on the edge of the bed and took my hand in his. "Perhaps it would be a good idea for us to visit the meditation center this afternoon."

"I'm sorry, but do you honestly believe meditation will help?" I knew I sounded like a bitch, but I'd never been a big believer in Tryst's "hocus-pocus."

"I believe the mind is a powerful instrument. Through focused thinking, we can achieve many things, Jada. Only if you imagine the life you desire, can you achieve it."

Now I felt like a bitch as much as I'd sounded like one. "I'm sorry," I repeated.

Tryst squeezed my hands. "Life is a journey, little one. The path you're intended to take will be of your own making."

I sat up, cringing when the movement made my chest feel as though it was on fire. However, that wasn't why my eyes filled with tears. "Are you saying what Al Zaabi did to me was of my own making?"

"You know I am not. How you heal from the trauma will be." He stood. "Let me know when you're ready, and we will go."

"Fuck!" I gasped when I closed my eyes and leaned back, hitting my head on the wall behind me. Then when I raised my hand to rub the hurt away, the pain in my chest intensified. Maybe I was a wimp. I had no way to gauge my threshold since I'd never been seriously injured before. The worst that had happened was a sprained ankle.

"Come in," I said when I heard a knock at the door.

"Is there anything you need?" Lynne asked.

Something that would stop me from *feeling*? A way to be invisible? Enough medication that I'd go to sleep and never wake up? I shook my head in response instead, then asked when I was due for more pain meds. She checked her watch.

"Another thirty minutes."

"Can you please let Tryst know I'll be ready to go after that?"

After telling me she would, Lynne closed the bedroom door behind her.

I reached over, picked up my cell phone, and swiped the screen. I had twenty-five text messages. I only read one, though. It was from Zin.

I miss you so fucking much I can't breathe.

10

Zin

Pain. It was ever present. Asleep or awake. Drunk or sober. Alone or with people. My mind occupied or staring off into space. No matter what, I ached.

After tossing and turning all night, not sleeping at all, I rolled out of bed and went downstairs. My dad was sitting at the table in the breakfast nook where my mom and I had sat yesterday.

"Where's Mom?" I asked.

"She went for a walk in the vineyards. These are among her favorites."

"Didn't feel like joining her?" I asked, pouring a cup of the coffee one of them had made.

"I wanted to talk to you."

"Can I get through this first?" I asked, motioning to the coffee.

"You can listen for now."

I needed caffeine even for that. "Go ahead," I said after I pulled out a chair and sat beside him.

"Martin Barrett mentioned Los Caballeros had weathered worse than what Onyx is threatening."

I blew on the steaming brew and took a sip.

"Back when Alfonso Avila was alive, we were targeted by a local attorney who'd actually defrauded Al out of a lot of money."

"Cooley?"

My dad's eyes widened. "You know the story?"

"Bits and pieces, but yeah, the gist of it."

"It was a rough time for the *caballeros*. For a while, we were certain Cooley would end us." He smiled. "We weren't smart enough to get Burns involved. The point is, we beat him at his own game. Not only did we survive, but he was indicted on multiple charges and went to prison."

"His son tried to pick up where he left off."

"This is news."

"Ridge's wife was an assistant district attorney. He blackmailed her to get dirt on us. Coincidentally, he was indicted on the same number of charges his dad was."

"The point is, there will always be those who threaten us. However, what can they really charge us with outside of obstruction of justice? In Onyx's case,

Burns has our backs. Even if he didn't, would it ever truly come to individual charges? I highly doubt it."

"I appreciate everything you're saying. My reason for offering my resignation had nothing to do with Onyx, though. It was more that some of the members, as well as the guys from K19, took issue with my actions. And, Dad, if I found out Jada was in any kind of danger now or in the future, I'd act the same way I did with Al Zaabi. Nothing and no one would change my response, even if it means I'll spend the rest of my life in prison."

"I feel the same way about you and your mother."

"No one would be surprised to hear it. In fact, I'm sure Doc would react the same way I did if his wife or kids were in danger. The difference here is no one knows about Jada and me. More people do now as opposed to a week ago. However, even Onyx is in the dark about her and me."

"Why? Especially now."

"It isn't up to me, Dad. He's Jada's brother. The decision to tell him is hers and hers alone."

"You care enough about her to risk yourself and Los Caballeros. Is that what you're saying?"

I looked out at the lawn where I'd lain the night before, waiting to see a second shooting star. If I had, I would've had a hard time deciding on a wish. Obviously, if wishes could change the past, it would have been that Jada was never abducted. "I'm sorry, but it is."

"Nothing to be sorry about. I'd be disappointed if you looked at it any other way." He studied me. "What are you thinking about?"

"I saw a shooting star last night."

He rested his head on his hand. "Did you make a wish?"

"I forgot."

"I think it counts for up to twenty-four hours after you see it."

I chuckled. "You sound like Mom."

He nodded. "We've been together a long time."

"I can't decide what to wish for."

"Jada. Wish for Jada."

That much was obvious. What I couldn't decide was whether to wish for her to get better regardless of whether I was part of her life or not, or to wish she'd let me be with her while she healed.

"Her wish, Dad? Or my own?"

"Meaning?"

"She wants me to back off and leave her alone."

"What is your wish, son?"

"I want to fight for her."

"Let's ask your mom," he said just as the door opened and she came inside.

"Ask me what?"

"Does Vaile respect Jada's wish to be left alone, or does he fight for her?"

She didn't hesitate. "Fight for her."

"What if I lose her?" I put my head in my hands to hide my tears.

My mom stood behind me, leaned over, and wrapped her arms around my shoulders. "What if you don't?"

I got up from the table and went outside. I walked over to the spot where I lay the night before. "My wish is for Jada to heal and for her to let me help her," I said out loud before pulling my phone from my pocket. I swiped the screen and typed a message to her.

I miss you so fucking much I can't breathe.

After waiting several minutes for a response that didn't come, I took a walk through the same rows of vines my mother had. Growing grapes was in my blood, passed down through generations. The first Olivers who did so were from France. We still owned vineyard property there, enough to make a few hundred cases each year.

In the late eighteen-sixties, my fifth great-grandfather immigrated to the United States and began purchasing property, first in Napa Valley, then on the Central Coast, where twenty years later, he began replacing apple orchards with grapevines. Some credited him with establishing the area's wine region.

It wasn't expected that I'd be an attorney like my dad; I'd just fallen in love with law. Lately, though, I'd become less enamored, maybe because it was something Jada and I argued about endlessly. Her reason for wanting to be a lawyer was the polar opposite of mine. Jada was entirely altruistic, while I was all about making money—something she'd hammered me about.

I checked my phone even though it hadn't vibrated. Jada still hadn't responded, but there was a text from Press, asking me to "ring" him.

"What's up?" I asked when he answered.

"Do you have a few minutes? I'd like to swing by."

I wasn't in the mood for company. In fact, I planned to convince my parents to return to Napa this afternoon.

"Can't whatever it is be handled over the phone?"

"It cannot."

"If it's about Jada—" I stopped talking when I heard the chimes indicating the call had ended.

By the time I got back to the house, he'd arrived.

"You hung up before I could say that if this is about Jada, you're wasting your time."

He sighed, and his eyes scrunched. "I gave you my apology for not telling you she was leaving for Mexico."

"I didn't accept it."

"Zin—"

I held up my hand. "Save it, Press, and think about how you'd feel if I'd whisked Luisa away without your knowledge."

"I have conceded I was wrong."

I walked over to the porch and sat on the top step. "Why are you here?"

"To see how you're doing and to talk about Jada."

"I'm fine, and I'm unwilling to discuss her with you."

"Why not?"

My eyes bored into his. "Because it's none of your fucking business."

Press sat beside me. "As the closest thing you have to a brother—by your own admission—I beg to differ."

"I changed my mind. I no longer think of you that way."

The asshole laughed. "I've often thought the same thing about Beau. Alas, it doesn't work that way."

"He *is* your brother."

Press put his hand on my shoulder. "As are you. I will not allow you to push me away. Nor would you allow me to if the situations were reversed."

"Thanks to you, I didn't get to say goodbye to Jada. I'm not welcome at the ranch, and she isn't responding to my messages. I'm going to hold a grudge for a long time."

"Have you tried contacting Tryst?"

I shook my head. Since he was the one who'd told me I wasn't welcome, why would I have bothered?

"I believe Doc's suggestion that Los Caballeros lie low for the time being is a good one. Perhaps the same is true for you and Jada."

"It isn't the same thing. Not even remotely so."

"Agreed."

I turned and looked at him. "Then, why the fuck did you say it?"

"I'm trying to open a dialogue."

I rested my elbows on my knees and put my head in my hands. "Why can't anyone understand I'm not interested in talking about Jada?"

"Those close to you know you need to."

"We didn't have a relationship, Press. We fucked when we felt like it. Okay? I've come to realize she meant more to me than I did to her. My fault for not keeping my feelings within the parameters we'd agreed upon."

"Are you willing to give up so easily?"

"Easily?" I shouted. "She's in Mexico. What am I supposed to do? Fly down there and shoot my way onto the ranch?"

"You have two choices. You can walk away, or you can fight for her."

"I just had the same conversation with my parents. I doubt you have insight different than theirs."

Press looked out at the horizon. "See that?" he asked, pointing.

"Fucking coyotes," I muttered. I'd spent over a hundred grand last year repairing the damage they'd done to my drip irrigation system.

"Odd she's on her own."

"How do you know it's a female?"

Press shrugged. "I suppose I don't."

The animal looked in our direction, then took off into the woods.

"Perhaps the best thing for now is to be patient. Believe me, I faced the same struggle with Luisa."

Same? Again, it wasn't. Back then, he barely knew her. They hadn't been sleeping together for four years. Hell, she was interested in Beau, not Press. The other difference was he saw her every single day. As friends, but still.

"I'm not suggesting you give up, Zin. I'm suggesting you back off for now."

"Is that all you came by to talk about? Because I feel like the record is skipping."

"Luisa and I are returning to Napa."

I stood. "Safe travels."

He got up too. "I'll be in touch, and if I hear anything about Jada, I'll keep you informed."

"See ya," I said before walking through my front door. It was the first time Press and I had parted ways for what could be an extended period of time without the obligatory hug. I felt shitty about it, just not enough to turn around and make it right.

"Was that Press?" my mom asked when I returned to the kitchen, where she and my dad were making a late breakfast.

"He and Luisa are leaving for Napa today."

Her brow raised. "I would've liked to say hello to him—and goodbye, it appears."

"He was in a hurry."

"Would you like an omelet?" My dad was standing near the cooktop and plated one.

"No thanks. Not hungry. I'm going to see if I can get some rest. I didn't get much sleep last night."

"Come here, Vaile," my mom said before I could get out of the kitchen.

"What?"

She approached me since I didn't take a step in her direction. "You look like you need a hug." I stiffened when she embraced me. "This will get better, son. I know it doesn't seem like it now, but it will." She dropped her arms.

I nodded and walked out. The problem was, I didn't know what "better" meant.

Halfway up to my bedroom, I looked out the wall of windows in the stairwell and saw the coyote. This time, it was closer to the house, and I could swear its eyes met mine.

11

Jada

"I thought we were going to meditate, not exercise," I grumbled.

"Yoga and meditation go hand in hand," Tryst said, laying two mats on the carpeted floor.

"Do you think this is a good idea?" I motioned to my chest.

"There are poses we can do that will not hurt."

"You know this from experience?" I muttered under my breath.

"We will begin with Easy Pose, also called Sukhasana. This is the one most people associate with yoga." Tryst led me to the mat and helped me to the floor before sitting on his own. "Watch me, and do what I do."

When he stretched his legs in front of him, I did too.

"Now, cross your shins and flex your feet. Make sure your knees are not higher than the level of your hips."

I folded my legs into the position I'd seen others do.

"Lengthen your torso as much as you can without causing pain. Your goal is to keep your chest from caving in. Next, bring your hands to heart center."

I slouched slightly when I felt my skin pull, then raised my hands.

"We will meditate in this position for a minimum of ten minutes. Close your eyes and focus on breathing. If you find your mind wandering, refocus on the point exactly between inhaling and exhaling. Once you are able to harness your thoughts, keep your attention focused solely on the present. What sounds do you hear? What do you smell? Do you feel warm or cold?"

My mind drifted, but as soon as I realized it had, I pushed myself to become hyperaware of the things Tryst mentioned. First, my breathing. Once I was able to do that, I listened for other things. The harder I concentrated, the more I could hear. Birds singing, initially. But then I could hear horses. Whinnies and the sound of their hooves.

My eyes sprung open. I lowered my hands and hugged my torso as chills spread throughout my body. I looked over at Tryst, who was studying me.

"Tell me what just happened."

"I heard a whip."

"Slow your breathing."

My eyes filled with tears. "I can't, Tryst. I have to get out of here."

He got up, then sat in front of me. "Focus your attention on me, Jada. Match your breathing to mine. Keep your eyes open." Tryst reached out and took my hands in his.

His exaggerated breaths were all I could hear. "Be present, little one. Stay here with me."

Could he read my mind? Did he know all I could see, eyes open or closed, was Al Zaabi raising his whip? I shuddered and fought back nausea.

"Look at our hands." Tryst squeezed my fingers, and I tried to pull away.

"It hurts."

He nodded and squeezed harder.

"*What are you doing?* I said that hurts."

"I'm bringing you back to the present," he said, easing his grip.

I watched the rise and fall of his chest, seeing only that. Each time my mind drifted, I brought it back.

"It will get easier each day as long as you are purposefully mindful."

"It's hard."

Tryst nodded. "Harder still to be patient in and with the process. You have done well today. I'm proud of you."

"Why do I think you'd say that even if I'd only lasted a minute?"

He smiled and squeezed my hands a last time before letting them go. "I was proud the moment you agreed to join me here. It took great courage."

I turned my head toward the window. "I'm not brave."

"As the great John Wayne said, 'Courage is being scared to death…and saddling up anyway.'"

"I heard horses."

"We keep many on the ranch as part of a training-and-rehabilitation program Rosa and I developed many years ago."

"Horse rehabilitation?"

"Yes, much of our work is centered on the animals themselves. We also facilitate equine-assisted psychotherapy."

I'd ask if it was something I could do, since I loved horses and had ridden most of my life. However, it was the sound of a whip that had sent me circling the drain.

I'd never used one myself, and even thinking about the poor animals being abused in that way made me ill.

"Tell me what you're thinking," he said like he did so often.

"I don't approve of whipping them."

"Neither do I."

I shook my head hard enough I felt the pull in my chest. "I heard it."

"However, you have no context in terms of its use."

"It doesn't matter, Tryst."

"If I give you my word that you won't see or hear another whip or any other kind of implement that would cause harm, will you accompany me to the riding center?"

As terrified as I was, I trusted Tryst. He would not give his word lightly. "When?"

"Now."

His response triggered me almost as badly as hearing the whip had. "I need to sit down." I couldn't catch my breath as chills ran from the tips of my fingers, up my arms, and down each side of my body.

Rather than focus on my breathing or Tryst's, I watched the beads of sweat from my forehead land in plops on the yoga mat just like they had on the cold concrete floor of the radio station. I covered my ears with my hands when their sound became deafening.

"Focus on my breathing, little one." I heard Tryst's words as though they were being spoken from somewhere far away rather than right in front of me.

I tried, but my eyes stung from the sweat trickling into them, distracting me. I squeezed them closed.

"I can't," I whispered.

When Tryst pulled me into his arms, I tried to fight, but I didn't have the strength. Instead, I sobbed as he held me on his lap and rocked—just like my daddy used to. "Shh," he whispered again and again, stroking my hair. Eventually, he carried me out of the meditation center and to the golf cart we'd arrived in earlier in the day. By the time we got to the house, the sun had set.

"What can I do?" I heard Lynne ask when she opened the door and Tryst swept through it with me once again in his arms.

"Help me get her out of these clothes and into a warm bath," he said, setting me on the bed.

"The pain…" I managed to say before my eyes closed and I slipped out of consciousness.

When I woke, sunlight was streaming through the windows and Tryst was sleeping in a chair by the bed, just like he had when I was at Butler Ranch.

The door opened, and Lynne eased through it when our eyes met.

"He was up with you all night," she whispered.

Tryst opened his eyes, sat up, and scrubbed his face with his hand.

"Please go get some sleep," I said, reaching for him when he stood.

"How are you this morning?"

"Better." I bit my lip. "I'm sorry about yesterday."

He leaned down and kissed my forehead. "Do not apologize. There is no need."

"I lost it."

"It is part of the process, little one." He looked up at Lynne. "Will you be okay if I sleep a while?"

"I'll kick your butt if you don't."

He chuckled and left the room.

"What happened last night after we returned to the house?"

"In a nutshell, you passed out. Tryst had one of the other women who work on the ranch come to the house to help me get you out of your clothes and into pajamas. It wasn't easy. You were drenched in sweat."

"I'm sorry," I said to her like I had to Tryst.

"Don't be. As your uncle said, it's part of the healing process. What you suffered mentally and emotionally will be harder to recover from than your physical wounds."

"Did Tryst tell you what happened at the meditation center?"

"A little. Enough to get the picture."

I nodded and rested my head on the pillow.

"How would you rate your pain?"

"Eight."

"I also have something to help with anxiety."

I opened my eyes and watched the needle penetrate my skin, sending medication coursing through my bloodstream. "He's not really my uncle," I whispered. "Tryst, I mean."

"I know." Lynne checked my pulse and oxygen, then took my blood pressure. "Try to sleep now. I'll be right here if you need anything."

"You don't have to—" I was out cold before I finished my sentence.

I was sitting in the kitchen with Lynne when Tryst walked in. It was early afternoon, and I'd spent the last couple of hours thinking about everything that happened the day before, wondering why I'd reacted the way I had.

"Did you get some rest?" I asked.

"Will you excuse us?" he said to Lynne rather than answer me. She left, and he sat in her chair. His brow was furrowed, almost as if he was in pain.

"Are you okay?"

"I'm sorry for pushing you yesterday. There is no timeline to healing."

"You're wrong now. You weren't then."

His eyes scrunched.

"If you don't push me, who will?"

"The progress you make at working through your recovery will be up to you, little one."

"Will you take me to the meditation center?"

I saw a hint of a smile. "When?"

"Now?" Yesterday, those two simple words had sent me into a tailspin; however, then we'd been talking about visiting the riding center. I took a deep breath before asking my next question. "You said something yesterday about the context of how the whips I heard were used."

He nodded, and any smile I might have seen, disappeared. "Yes," he responded.

"How are they used, Tryst?"

"When you are ready, it will be better for you to see."

"You won't tell me?"

"I will not."

12

Zin

"I don't need you two to stay here. You can go home."

My parents looked at each other, and both laughed.

"What's funny?"

"You were never one to beat around the bush," my dad said at the same time the waiter brought the bottle of wine he'd ordered.

My mom covered my hand with hers. "We'd like to stick around a while longer."

"You're welcome to, of course. I just…"

"Want to be alone," my father finished my sentence.

"I am a grown man."

He shook his head and looked at my mom.

"What?" I demanded.

"Regardless of age, you need a support network. Everyone does, Vaile," she responded.

What I needed was time to think. I had decisions to make, and all I did was vacillate. I went back and forth between knowing I had to accept Jada and I were fin- ished and wanting to fly to Mexico and work things out between us. My decision would have been made easier if she'd responded to my text. Her radio silence left me feeling as though I was an idiot for believing there was anything to work out.

There was another realization I'd come to, and once I had, I felt a profound sense of relief. I was shutting down my law practice. The only exception would be if someone from Los Caballeros needed legal help. Otherwise, I was done.

"I'll renew my license to practice every year; however, I'm retiring from the law," I announced. "Except for the *caballeros*."

Neither of my parents appeared surprised.

"I'm going to focus my efforts on the winery here in Paso Robles. I'll also help out more in Napa."

My dad gave me a head nod.

"No comments?"

"If you believe this is the right course of action for you, of course your mother and I will support it."

"I don't love it like I used to," I said more to myself than to them. There was a chance I'd change my mind, but right now, I didn't see that happening.

"What about Jada?"

"I don't know yet, Mom."

"You should reach out to Tryst, at least to express your concern. There's nothing inappropriate in inquiring about her well-being. He's certainly aware of your involvement in her rescue."

It dawned on me that the last time I talked to Jada, it was because Tryst had offered to "stand watch" in the event Onyx showed up. Maybe I was looking at his involvement wrong. What he'd said was, "If she wants you to accompany her, then by all means, you should." That was much different than him saying I wasn't welcome.

"I feel as though you've had an epiphany."

"Maybe I have. Thanks, Mom." I excused myself from the table, went outside, and sent Tryst a simple and innocuous message.

How is Jada doing?

A few seconds later, he responded. *She is struggling.*

Can I help?

I will let you know when the time comes you can.

While I wanted to ask when he thought that would be, I didn't. I knew Tryst well enough to be sure that if he had a timeline in mind, he would've said so. Just that he'd said "when the time comes" made me feel better.

When I returned to our table, I felt optimistic. I couldn't remember the last time I had.

Evidently, my parents recognized it since the next morning, they announced they were leaving.

"Say the word, and we'll get here as quickly as we can," my mom said, tearing up when we hugged.

"Ditto." My dad and I also embraced.

As I watched their car pull away from the house, I thought about how if they'd left yesterday, I would've pulled out a fresh bottle of Scotch and drowned myself in it. Instead, I took a walk in the vineyard.

To some, the leafless rows of vines might look bleak. However, what was occurring beneath the surface of the wood was vital to the success of the growing period that would soon follow.

"Good to see you out here," said Tomahawk "Tommy" Brant, the head viticulturist—or vineyard manager—for our family's properties on the Central Coast. Few knew, but Tommy had given me the nickname Zin.

While some wineries preferred to employ two people in his position, our family had always believed the ratio of one vineyard expert and one head winemaker made for more consistent wine.

I approached and shook his hand. "How are you, sir?"

"These old bones are gnarlier than the vines in twelve." I remembered thinking Tomahawk—which he swore was his real name—was an old man when I was a kid. He didn't appear much different now than he had then. According to his employment record, he was nearly eighty.

The plot he referred to was where our oldest rootstock grew—Zinfandel. "What are you checking today?"

"Chardonnay."

"Can I be your shadow?"

He smiled and cuffed me like he had when I was ten years old and followed him wherever he went.

It was a long walk to where we grew Chardonnay, and I was relieved to see Tommy had a golf cart parked near the edge of the plot we were in. For years, he'd refused to use one.

"You're unsettled," he said after climbing into the passenger seat and motioning for me to drive.

"I'm retiring."

Tommy looked out at the vineyards we passed. "That isn't it."

"It's Jada."

"I see."

"Something happened to her."

He nodded. "I spoke with your father."

"Did he tell you about her and me?"

Tommy smiled. "He did not, nor did I divulge your secret."

He was one of the only people who knew about her and me and how long we'd been seeing each other. There were probably other vineyard workers who'd seen her come and go throughout the years, but Tommy was the only person I'd talked to about her.

"How is she?" he asked.

"Not well." I stopped the cart and pointed off in the distance at a coyote looking out at us from the ridge. We were too far away from it for me to know whether it was the same one I'd seen with Press and later on my own. "See that?"

"What?"

I looked again, and it was gone. "Coyote. Third time I've seen one on its own in as many days."

"What have you learned?"

"What do you mean?"

"My people, the Miwoks, believe seeing a coyote is a sign of spiritual significance."

"I'm supposed to learn something from it?" The last thing I wanted to do was insult Tommy, but the only thing I'd learned was to keep an eye on our irrigation system.

"Open your mind, Zin. Then you'll recognize the lessons."

I spent the rest of the afternoon helping Tommy mark which vines needed to be pruned. We wouldn't begin the actual work until the beginning of February, but given how long of a process it was, we used this period of dormancy to plan for the months ahead.

Rather than take him up on his offer of a ride to the house, I told Tommy I'd prefer to walk. While I kept my head down for most of the way, mainly because I didn't want to see the coyote I was beginning to think was stalking me, I raised my head when I heard a car on the gravel. Only a select few had the code to my gate, so when I saw Brix's truck, I wasn't all that surprised.

"Hey," I said when he climbed out.

"Hey."

"Everything okay?" I studied him. Brix was a hard one to figure out. He almost always looked like something was wrong. Although that had changed over the past few months, since he and Addy got married.

"Just stoppin' in to say hello and see how you're doing."

"Are you Press' stand-in?"

He cocked his head.

"My babysitter?"

He shook his head but laughed. "You're an asshole."

"Seriously. Why are you here?"

"You may have forgotten I'm one of your best friends, but I haven't."

"Sorry, man. I'm just…"

"A fucking mess."

This time, I laughed. "That's accurate."

"Are you gonna invite me in for a drink, or are we gonna stand out here in your driveway?"

I motioned for him to follow me inside. "Wine, beer, Scotch?"

"Let's cut straight to the good stuff."

I pulled a bottle out of the pantry in the kitchen and poured two fingers into the glasses Brix handed to me. "My guess is everyone's asking about you and Jada."

I carried the bottle of booze and my glass into the living room. Brix followed, and we took a seat. "If that means our relationship is common knowledge, things just got a *helluva* lot worse for me."

He took a sip of his drink. "I never thought I'd say this, but a man in love recognizes when his friends are too."

"It wasn't that kind of relationship."

He chuckled. "My sister used to say that about her and Maddox Butler."

"What you're looking at is a man whose feelings are not reciprocated."

He stood and walked over to the windows that looked out over the vineyards. "Jada might not be an Avila, but she's definitely a Ramirez."

I got up too and joined him. "What's that mean?"

"My mother and Jada's are twins. Their maiden name was Ramirez."

I poured another two fingers for myself and motioned to his glass.

"I guess Addison won't be too mad at me if she has to come drive me home. She's the one who pushed me out the door."

"Yeah? Getting on her nerves?"

"More that she's worried about you, Zin."

"Fuck," I said under my breath. "Please tell her not to be." I raised my eyes, and damn, if that coyote wasn't back.

I pointed to it. "Tomahawk said that mangy creature out there is a spirit sent to teach me a lesson."

"Tryst used to say that too. Or something like that. He believes coyotes help guide us on our journeys."

"Damn. Good thing there's a no-kill ban on them, or there'd be a lot of stuck people in the world." I shook my head.

After we sat back down, I told Brix what I'd said to my dad about giving up being an attorney and that I planned to spend more time on day-to-day vineyard operations.

"Yeah? That's good news because I came to ask for your help with something."

"Of course. Something legal?"

Brix shook his head. "Actually, I was wondering if you'd have time to head down to Mexico with Addy and me. Since the weather's been nice, I'm hoping to make some progress on our house."

The house Brix referred to was the one he was building on the property Tryst had given him and Addy as a wedding gift. Five thousand acres adjacent to *El Lugar de Curación* Ranch. "Are you serious?"

"We're talking about leaving in the morning. Think you can be ready by then?"

"Are you sure this is a good idea?"

"From what I remember, you weren't half bad with a hammer back when you helped Tryst and me with my house here."

"Does your uncle know you invited me?"

Brix grinned. "My house. My property, Zin."

"If you're sure."

"Somebody had to throw you a bone to get you down there. You aren't any good to Jada from two thousand miles away."

"I won't be any good to her as close as two miles if she won't see me."

"Look at it this way; if she does decide she wants to, you can show up at her front door before she has a chance to change her mind."

13

Jada

"Where is the riding center?" I asked the next morning when we were in the golf cart on our way to the meditation room.

Tryst pointed. "Just over that ridge."

"Very far?"

He shook his head. "Quite close, actually."

I loved horses. I'd been riding them my whole life. Our family didn't own them, but our cousins, the Avilas, did. My mom loved to take us there since it meant she got to spend time with her sister, Lucia Avila.

There was nothing like the freedom of riding a horse, especially in a place like this, where I was sure there were endless trails to explore.

I looked over to where he pointed, then took a deep breath. "Can I see it?"

Tryst stopped the cart. "Are you certain, Jada?"

I put my hand on his arm. The look on his face was so like the earlier one, when he'd seemed almost tortured about the role he played in my meltdown. "I am. Please take me there."

He put the cart back in gear and turned in the direction he'd pointed. When we crested the hill, I asked him to stop.

"This is it, isn't it? Where you and Rosa walked to that first day? Can we get out?"

"Of course." The smile on Tryst's face almost brought me to tears. I couldn't imagine how much he missed his late wife. As hard as I tried not to think about Zin, I missed him too. Terribly. Tryst's pain must have felt a thousand times worse.

"This is the El Palomar valley, right?" I couldn't imagine any other view would be as sweeping or as beautiful.

"It is. If you look that way, you'll see our home."

"It looks so far away from here, yet we were only driving a few minutes."

"And there is the riding center." Like his earlier smile, the pride in his voice made me emotional.

He pointed almost directly below us. It was so much bigger than I'd expected. There were four barns, each with an adjacent corral. Beyond that was a large pasture that appeared endless, but I could just make out a fence line. There had to be at least one hundred horses grazing.

"You said you run a rehabilitation program?"

"We keep the horses separated by their trauma levels and recovery rate. As they improve, we move between barns. Eventually, they'll transition to the freedom of the pasture."

"Where do they come from?"

"At first, it was only from Mexico, but as our reputation spread, people began bringing them from the States. Many of them come via rescue organizations."

"What happens to them when they leave?"

Tryst sat on the grass and motioned for me to join him. "Many live the rest of their lives here. Some return to the people who brought them here. Others are adopted."

"It's a good thing you do, Tryst."

"Rosa was passionate about all animals, but horses especially. She was so good with them. The ranch hands called her the whisperer." He chuckled. "This was long before the book and movie." When his eyes scrunched and his brow furrowed, I followed his line of sight.

"What's wrong?"

"They will be doing a demonstration very soon."

"Of what?"

"Trust."

"It involves the whip, doesn't it?"

He stood and held his hand out to me. "Come, we'll be on our way."

I got up but didn't follow when he walked toward the golf cart. "I want to see it."

Tryst returned to where I stood and put his hands on my shoulders. "It was the sound that affected you so profoundly yesterday, little one."

"You said it was something I had to see to understand." I grasped his hand. "I want to."

"If it is too much—"

"You said they aren't used on the horses."

"They are not. I promise you. They are not used to hit anything at all." He pointed again. "Watch the cowboy."

Even from here, I could see the whip in the man's hand as he mounted a horse that stood perfectly still in the middle of the corral. I was astonished to see the cowboy stand, balancing himself on the saddle.

Tryst moved closer to me. "Watch the horse."

It was all I could do not to reach up and plug my ears when the man raised the whip. I blinked away the tears that filled my eyes, keeping them focused as much as I could on the animal. I could hear the whip crack, but the horse didn't flinch. The cowboy raised his arm once more, and this time, I watched him instead. The whip hit the ground, not enough to raise any dust. Again, the horse didn't appear to move a muscle.

The man shifted on the saddle, moving just slightly. Every few inches, he'd crack the whip again, and while it got close to the horse, it didn't touch it. Nor did the horse move.

"When the horse arrived at the ranch, she was severely malnourished. She'd been horribly abused for years."

"Whipped?" I asked, tears now streaming down my cheeks.

"Yes," Tryst said, squeezing my hand. "But now, she no longer fears she'll be hurt. She trusts."

I lowered my head and cried openly. "How long has she been here, Tryst?"

"A few weeks."

The cowboy lowered himself to a sitting position and maneuvered the horse over to the corral's gate. When it opened, a woman approached them, and the man dismounted. He handed her the reins, and with her other hand, she wiped her face, then mounted and took the animal through several paces in the enclosed area.

"Does she belong to her?" I asked.

"I believe she might one day very soon."

I leaned over and rested my head on his shoulder. "You're a good man, Tryst."

He turned so he could look into my eyes. "My life has not always been easy, little one. I have suffered more than you'll ever know—physically, emotionally, mentally, even spiritually. Some days remain difficult, but through meditation, prayer, and taking care of my body as well as my soul, I can smile, be happy, and celebrate the purpose of my life."

"I envy you," I whispered when the tears that had abided began to fall again.

He shook his head. "You will find your way, Jada. You are not as lost as you think."

"Are people able to ride any of them?" I asked.

"Of course."

"I'd like to."

"Will tomorrow be soon enough? There's something else I'd like to show you."

"Tomorrow will be fine." I stood and realized Tryst was studying me.

"What?" I asked, looking down at my clothes.

"You have the most beautiful smile, little one. It fills my heart with happiness."

I had to admit it felt really good to me too. "What is this?" I asked when Tryst pulled the golf cart up to a conical-shaped building made of brick but painted to look like marble.

"This is the temple. Come." Tryst led me up large stones and pulled open a wooden door. He took my hand, and we walked to the very center of the space. "Look up."

There were what looked like a hundred or more small skylights built into the steeple.

"Close your eyes and receive," said Tryst, dropping my hand. On instinct, I held my arms out in front of me at an angle and turned my wrists so my palms were up.

The sun's warmth washed over me, but it felt like more than that. I slowly turned in a circle as if I was wrapping myself in its blanket. I could feel tears running down my cheeks, but I wasn't sad. Instead, I felt at peace. When I opened my eyes, Tryst was seated in one of the pews. His eyes bored into mine, and he smiled. I walked over and sat beside him.

"How do you feel?" he asked.

"I don't think I have words to explain."

"No need. It happens to me every time I visit."

"I would never want to leave." I closed my eyes, taking it all in, thinking about how nice it would be to bundle up my feelings and carry them out of the temple with me, when the sense of something entirely different washed over me.

My eyes sprung open, and I looked at Tryst.

"What is it?"

"Zin."

"What about him?"

"This is another thing I can't explain, but I've always been able to *feel* when he was near." I wrapped my arms around my stomach. "Tryst, is Zin here?"

"He is not, Jada. I would not invite him to the ranch without your permission. More, without you asking me to issue the invitation."

"You're sure?"

"I heard from him the night before last. He asked how you were doing, and I told him the truth, that you are struggling. He wanted to know if there was anything he could do to help."

"What did you say?"

"That if and when the time came he could, I would let him know."

"Zin and I have been seeing each other."

"I gathered it was something like that."

I longed to return to the warmth under the steeple. "In secret. For four years."

"That is a long time to keep a secret. Why did you?"

"To be honest, I don't remember. I guess I thought Zin preferred no one know."

"You guess?"

It seemed ridiculous now that we'd never actually talked about it. Or if we had, it had been back in the beginning.

"He means a great deal to you."

I shrugged. "He does. I won't lie. I need to let him go, though."

He cocked his head but didn't speak.

"Things have changed. With me, I mean. Um, my body…"

He nodded slowly. "Do you believe Zin won't accept you as you look now?"

"Not just that. The memories, the dreams—"

"You call out for him in your sleep."

It took me a minute to process Tryst's words. "I do? Really?"

"Lynne will confirm it if you doubt me."

"I don't. It's just, um, surprising. Maybe confusing would be a better word."

He looked at his watch. "We should return to the house. It is getting close to the time for your next dose of medicine. It is important for you to stay ahead of the pain, little one."

The sun was bright enough when we walked out of the temple that I had to shield my eyes. I looked up the steep incline to my left and, at first, thought I saw a man standing at the top. I blinked, and it looked more like an animal. Maybe a coyote. I blinked a second time, and whatever it was—likely a figment of my imagination—was gone.

The odd sensation I'd always equated with feeling Zin close by stayed with me until I fell asleep. It was still there when I woke the next morning with no memory of having nightmares.

"Can we go to the riding center today?" I asked, coming into the kitchen, where Tryst sat.

"Good morning to you too, Jada."

"Sorry." My cheeks flushed. "Good morning, Tryst."

He chuckled. "You have always been so anxious to *do*." He emphasized his last word.

"Is that a nice way of saying I'm impatient?"

"Not at all. I've always loved your zest for life, little one. It is rare that I wish to be young again, but there have been times I thought it would be nice to relive my childhood with an outlook more like yours."

"Me too," I whispered. As hard as I tried not to, my eyes filled with tears. I hated how often it happened.

"Jada—"

I held up my hand. "I don't want to talk about it. Can we please just go ride?"

"Absolutely."

"I thought I heard voices. Good morning," said Lynne, coming out of her bedroom. "Where are you off to?"

"Horseback riding."

Her eyes opened wide. "Are you feeling up to it?"

"Right now, I do. Maybe just some ibuprofen today?"

"You got it." She went to the bedroom and returned a minute later. After she handed me the pills, I took them with a glass of water.

"Are you sure you don't want something to eat before you go?" she asked.

Tryst laughed. "She wouldn't be able to sit still long enough to eat it. She's been that way since she was a little girl. I remember your siblings would get so mad when your papa let you leave the table without finishing your supper. He always had a soft spot for you."

"Wow. I don't remember that."

"I'm sure your brothers and sisters do."

My bravado was short-lived once we reached the barns. My chest throbbed just thinking about using the muscles it would take to pull myself up and throw my leg over the horse that was saddled up and ready for me.

"This might make it easier," said one of the cowboys, bringing over a mounting block. I had never had to use one, from what I could remember. It felt like I was being forced to ride a bike with training wheels.

"I can do it," I insisted.

"Can I help?" he asked, stepping closer.

"No!" God, why had I just shouted at the guy? "Sorry. I'll, um, just use the block."

Even that hurt, but once I was in the saddle, hands on the reins, heels down in the stirrups, I forgot all about the pain. I eased Berta into a walk. "Sorry about your name, girl," I said, rubbing her neck. In return, she gave me a short, low whinny.

The cowboy who'd brought over the block opened the gate. Just outside, Tryst waited, seated in the saddle of one of the most beautiful horses I'd ever seen. "Is that a Friesian?" I asked, admiring its shiny black coat and long, arched neck. One clue to the animal's breed was the silky hair—known as feathers—on its lower legs that had been deliberately left untrimmed.

Tryst nodded. "This is Brutus. He and Berta were raised together."

I rolled my eyes. "Unfortunate name choices on both accounts."

"Thank you."

My cheeks flushed. "No, Tryst, tell me it wasn't you."

He laughed. "It wasn't. However, I had no desire to rename them."

While both horses were docile, neither lacked energy or a willingness to go where we led them.

"What's up there?" I asked when I looked to my left and saw a figure standing where I thought I had seen someone last night.

Tryst looked where I pointed. "Ah, Brix and Addison are here. They're building a house not far from where he stands."

"You can tell it's him?" I asked.

"It's his property, and I know how anxious they are to complete construction."

Maybe that's why I sensed Zin's presence. He and my cousin had been almost inseparable since they were kids.

"Would you like to go farther, or shall we turn back?" Tryst asked when we'd been riding for about an hour.

"I'd say farther, but it's been a long time since I've been in the saddle."

"This trail will get us to the riding center." He pointed to one slightly lower than what we were on.

That night, before I fell asleep, I allowed my mind to drift to Zin. When I woke the following day, I couldn't recall having any nightmares.

It became my routine, and as long as I went to sleep thinking about him, the nightmares stayed at bay.

Tryst gradually left me on my own more over the course of the next couple of days. I appreciated the solitude as well as the freedom. I visited the temple, lingered at the meditation center, and rode out. When alone, I didn't venture as far on B, as I'd nicknamed the sweet horse I was growing attached to.

While my legs were definitely getting stronger, my upper body wasn't, which meant I had to use the mounting block. When I complained about my lack of progress, Tryst showed me yoga poses I could do to strengthen my core yet not strain the chest wounds that were still healing.

B and I were returning to the barn when she snorted. I could feel her tense beneath me and looked ahead on the trail. A lone coyote stood a few feet away. I looked around and breathed a sigh of relief when I didn't see others. That it was off on its own likely meant it was old, injured, or both.

"Don't be afraid," I said, patting B's neck and slowing her. "Your thousand pounds could easily crush its forty." We'd almost come to a standstill when the coyote ran off down the sloping hillside. "See? It was more afraid of us than we were of it." However, it left me feeling unsettled enough that I continued to glance over my shoulder on our ride back.

"How was your ride?" asked the cowboy who'd helped me the first day and whose name I'd learned was Tex.

"B and I had a near run-in with a coyote, but it took off before she got too spooked."

"There are a lot of them around these parts."

"I'm going to try to dismount on my own today," I told him when he held out his hand.

"I'm here if needed," he said, taking a single step back.

I gathered the reins in my left hand and placed it above B's withers. After putting my right hand below the pommel, I removed my right foot from the stirrup, bending my leg and moving it over B's croup.

I was about to move my right hand to the cantle when I realized my mistake. To safely dismount, I'd have to slide myself down B's side, and I had no doubt it would hurt like a *sonuvabitch* if I did.

"Help," I said, glancing over my shoulder, my left foot still in the stirrup.

"I got you," said Tex, putting both hands on my waist and pulling back far enough that the front of my body wouldn't graze the horse's side.

"Thanks," I said when my feet landed on the ground.

"I'll take care of B today," Tex said when I was about to lead her into the barn.

I thanked him rather than argue. It wasn't like our ride was particularly long or more strenuous than any other, yet I still felt fatigued. I shuddered, also sensing I was being watched.

14

Zin

We'd arrived in Alamos five days ago, and I'd seen Jada a few times, all from a distance. There were moments I thought she'd seen me too. Well, maybe not me, but someone standing at the top of the hill that looked down on Tryst's ranch. Had she known who she was looking at, I had no doubt she would've reacted in some way. Most likely by sending Tryst to Brix's place to tell me I wasn't welcome here.

While Brix reminded me I was *his* guest on *his* property, if his uncle had come and asked me to vacate, I would've respected his wishes—or Jada's.

I still felt completely removed from her, as far away as if I was still in California. The only thing that assuaged my body's yearning for hers were the long days and nights Brix and I spent working on his house.

As difficult as the work was, it felt good. Like when I spent the day in the vineyard with Tomahawk, I felt a sense of renewal, of rejuvenation.

Each day when I woke, I was buoyed by the possibility that, sometime in the next few hours, I might see Jada again, maybe even from close enough to see her smile or tell her how much I missed her. How much she meant to me.

"I just ended a call with Tryst," said Brix, walking over to where I stood on the steep incline's precipice from where I watched for her. He approached and put his hand on my shoulder.

"And?"

"Your name didn't come up, if that's what you're asking."

I supposed that was good news. At least I wasn't about to be banished.

"He invited Addison and me to dinner tonight. I couldn't come up with a reason we shouldn't go."

"You definitely should."

"You're okay with it?"

I raised a brow. "That isn't even worthy of a response." I looked down at the corral when Jada rode up on the same horse she'd ridden every day since I arrived. "She's going to try to dismount," I said under my breath, wishing I could fly down the hill and stop her. It was too soon. She might even risk ripping open the wounds that had required sutures. She'd thrown one leg over when the cowboy who stood behind her stepped closer. My fists clenched at my sides, watching him put his hands on her waist and lift her from the horse. "Who is that?" I asked Brix, pointing.

"Looks like Tex."

"He had his hands on her," I mumbled.

"He helped her get off the horse. There's nothing more to it."

"You can't be sure."

Brix rubbed his chin. "Actually, I can. Tex, uh, gets on the horse from the opposite side."

As much as I didn't want to look away from the scene below, I cocked my head in his direction.

"Bats for the other team?"

"Are you trying to say he's gay, Brix?"

"Yeah. That."

I shook my head. "Are you seriously that unenlightened?"

"That isn't it. I'm just not sure what's okay to say these days and what's not."

My eyes opened wide. "With me? You're not sure what to say around me?" I laughed. "I'd take bets I am the least politically correct person you know. That you've ever known."

He chuckled. "My dad would've run a close second."

"Maybe he's bi," I muttered, watching the man lead the horse toward the barn and Jada walk in the opposite direction. She came to an abrupt stop, turned slowly, and looked in our direction. The sun was directly behind Brix and me at this time of day, so the most she'd see was our silhouettes. Within a second or two, she kept walking.

"Go to dinner. See how she's doing."

"What will you do?"

"Probably crack open that bottle of Mezcal you brought and get shit-faced."

"Just don't be hungover tomorrow. We're roofing the north section."

When I walked toward the house, he followed.

"You could go into town. There are a few places I could recommend for dinner."

I wasn't hungry and said so.

"All right. I'm gonna take a shower, then Addison and I are leaving."

"Have fun," I muttered and kept walking. There were endless trails I hadn't yet hiked that led to spectacular views. Plus, alone, I had uninterrupted time to think about Jada. Two weeks ago, I took it for granted that I could see her any time I wanted to. Now, there was a giant empty hole inside me, and I wondered if I would ever be full again.

Jada Yáñez had crawled into my heart when I wasn't looking—or paying attention—and that's where she'd live for the rest of my life.

It hurt like a motherfucker to think I was losing her. Physically hurt. It took something drastic, life-altering, and traumatic for me to realize I wanted to be with her more than anything in the world. *Anything.*

Love, fear, and pride mixed together in the rocks glass that was my life. I loved her. I was terrified I'd lost her. And yet, my pride kept me from taking the trail that led from Brix's house to Tryst's, banging on the door, and telling her how I felt.

We were both so young when this thing between us began. Each of us darting off in the opposite directions our lives took us but, somehow, always meeting back in the middle.

There were times I'd tried to run away from the passion between us. Times she did too. Maybe we were both afraid of what actual commitment might mean.

Fuck—what had I been afraid of? I wanted to pull my hair out at how goddamn clueless I'd been.

No one had ever made me feel the way Jada did. The almost-Shakespearean tragedy of that was I doubted I'd ever find it again.

When the sun began to set, I turned around. I knew enough landmarks to find my way during daylight but certainly not after dark. Once I reached the house, I walked into the kitchen, picked up the bottle of Mezcal like I'd told Brix I would, grabbed a glass, and went outside to watch the final vestiges of the sunset. I prayed it wasn't a metaphor for my relationship with Jada. Part of me would wither and die if it was, and that kept me awake at night.

I wished so hard I could ask her to come over here, lie with me, and let me hold her in my arms for a few minutes just so I could feel whole again. I'd throw away my pride and beg if she'd only talk to me.

The main reason I wouldn't push my way back into her life, though, was because it wasn't what *she* wanted. Jada's feelings meant more to me than mine. I was ashamed to think that, for the first time in my life,

I knew what putting the needs and desires of someone else before my own felt like.

I went into the room Brix and Addy had set up as a makeshift bedroom and lay on the mattress. How often had I wished I could travel back in time and do things differently? So many things.

But I couldn't, and with every passing day, my fear that Jada would forget about us—forget about me—intensified. I drank the rest of what was in my glass and stared up at the ceiling, tears rolling down each side of my face, and came to another realization. I couldn't give up yet. I couldn't risk her thinking I didn't care. At the very least, I had to reach out one more time.

I picked up my phone, brushed away the tears that continued to fall, and swiped the screen.

I love you, Jada, I wrote on our message thread. Then, letter by letter, deleted it before writing it again—over and over—until finally, I'd had enough of the agave liquor that I lay on the mattress that felt as though it was spinning, wishing it would magically transport me into her arms.

I woke sometime in the middle of the night and swiped the screen of my cell out of habit. It opened to our message thread, and to my horror, I saw that instead of hitting delete the last time I retyped my words, I'd sent them to her.

If nothing else, it proved what a fucking selfish bastard I was. Rather than think about her and how a message like that would come across via text, I'd sent it. Why? Because deep down, I believed it would make her respond and fill part of the giant hole inside of me. *Me.* I'd made it about me. *Again.* I was filled with self-loathing.

15

Jada

It was rude of me, but when I felt my cell phone vibrate, I excused myself from the table and walked into the bedroom to read the alert.

As foolish and unfair as it was, I prayed it was another message from Zin. Why would it be, though? I'd never answered the other he sent.

He'd been on my mind every waking minute of the past five days. He'd been in my dreams too. I couldn't shake the notion he was nearby. I'd thought seeing Brix might make the feeling go away, but it hadn't. It hadn't changed it at all.

I yearned for Zin, would give *almost* anything for him to come to Mexico, would beg him to hold me in his arms, beg him to make love to me. What held me back? I slowly unfastened the buttons of my shirt, stood in front of the mirror, and reminded myself. It was still too painful to wear a bra, not that I needed one with my B-cups, so when I pulled the sides of my blouse away and peeled off the dressing Lynne had replaced earlier, there was nothing to hide the reason I could never ask Zin to hold me or make love to me again.

I couldn't put either of us through the trauma of his reaction when he first saw what Al Zaabi did to me. He would be horrified, and that would devastate me.

The monster had held me captive a little over twenty-four hours. I knew that now, but when it was happening, it felt like days. In that time, the bastard had taken so much from me.

I'd lived most of the twenty-five years of my life without fear. The exceptions were when my brother was in a plane crash and we didn't know if he was alive. Then, when he was rescued, we weren't sure if he'd ever come out of the coma he was in.

I also experienced fear when Luisa was missing. I was terrified, like I had been with my brother, that I'd never see her again.

There had been pain. When my father died, especially. But I'd always held on to hope. Hope the anguish of losing him would fade. Hope Montano would recover. Hope Luisa would too.

Al Zaabi had stripped me of hope for myself, but that wasn't all. He'd taken away my confidence. My sense of who I was. And hardest of all, he'd taken away the love of my life. I loved Zin, even though I'd never told him I did.

It was another fear I hadn't realized I carried with me until now. Why hadn't I told him? Because I was afraid, if I did, he'd end things between us. He'd never said a word about our having a future beyond the next time we had sex. Not once.

Hope. A life without fear. My self-confidence. Who I was as a person. Love. *Zin.* Al Zaabi took all that from me.

It was why I'd told Zin I was mad that he killed the man. *I* wanted to be the one who took his life. I wanted vengeance. Maybe I hadn't realized it at the time, but that's what it was. I wanted to be the one who made the psychopath pay.

I wiped away my tears, fastened my blouse, and sat on the edge of the bed. Deep inside, I knew the text wasn't from him, and now that I'd processed through my feelings, I also knew it was for the best. Most likely, it was Luisa, my mom, or one of my siblings checking in. I swiped the phone's screen and gasped.

I love you, Jada, read the message.

God, why? Why now? Why did he have to say those words when there was no hope for us? No possibility we could ever be together again?

I lay on the bed and buried my face in the pillow to drown out the cry of anguish that built from a place deep inside me and sobbed.

I never returned to dinner. I couldn't. Eventually, Lynne came to check on me, and I feigned sleep. Once she shut the door, I swiped at my phone and studied Zin's message like I had been every minute since I first read it. He loved me. What did that even mean? Did he love me like a friend? Like someone he'd known most of his life? Or did he love me the way I loved him? The saddest part was I'd never know.

"Where's Tryst?" I asked the next morning when I found Lynne alone in the kitchen.

"There was an emergency with the horses, so he had to go to the riding center."

"What was the emergency? Did he say?"

She shook her head. "He didn't."

"How long has he been gone?"

Lynne looked at her watch. "About thirty minutes."

"I'll head there myself," I told her as I walked out the door and over to the golf cart Tryst had said was available for my use and drove to the barns.

There were very few cowboys out when I arrived. They were probably all helping Tryst with whatever the emergency was. When I saw Tex, I got out of the cart and walked over to him.

"I didn't expect to see you this early."

"I heard there was an emergency with the horses."

"A pack of coyotes managed to work their way into the pasture. One of the horses spooked and tripped on the fence wire. She may have a broken leg. Tryst and the vet are out there now."

When Tex lowered his head and shuffled his feet in the dirt, a feeling of dread overcame me.

"What aren't you saying?"

"Shit, Jada…"

"*What?*" I shouted. "Just tell me."

"It's Berta."

"Berta?" I cried. If Berta's leg was broken, there was a good chance the vet was here to put her down. I couldn't allow that to happen. *Couldn't.*

I turned in a circle, taking in the horses already saddled in the corral. I recognized one. It was the animal Tex had stood on the back of when he'd cracked the whip. I raced over to her when, from the corner of my eye, I saw the mounting block. I didn't have time for Tex to drag it over, and even if he did, he'd discourage me from riding out. It was as though everything around me was moving in slow motion as I ran to the horse, put my foot in the stirrup, and threw my leg over. "Open the gate!" I shouted at Tex.

Another cowboy beat him to it. As the horse and I flew past them, I heard Tex shouting.

"When you get to the three barrel cactus, go south. That's where the breach in the fence happened."

"C'mon, girl," I said. "Let's find, Berta." I eased her from a walk into a trot, then a canter, and finally, a full gallop. We didn't have far to go. In the distance, I could see four or five people crowded together, and a few feet ahead, I spotted the three barrel cactus.

"Wait!" I screamed as I got closer, praying I wasn't too late. The circle of men opened as I approached, and I saw Berta on the ground. Her eyes were open, and she was moving. I jumped off the horse whose name I didn't know and ran over, almost coming to a full stop

when my eyes met those of the last person I expected to see—Zin.

I looked from him to Berta. She had to come first. She needed me, at least to comfort her. My own comfort could wait. I knelt down beside her head and stroked her neck. "Hey, B. What did I tell you about riding out without me?" Tears streamed down my cheeks when I thought about how she'd spooked when we saw the lone coyote on the trail. "You must've been terrified," I leaned down and whispered. "I'm here now, B. I've got you." I looked up at Tryst. When he nodded, a man stepped forward. He held a large syringe.

"No! Not yet," I pleaded. "Not yet."

I felt two arms go around me, and I tried to jerk away. I didn't want comfort for me; I wanted it for B.

"Shh," whispered Zin. "It'll be okay. He's just going to sedate her so we can get her back to the barn without further injury." He smoothed my hair and kissed my cheek. "That's all, Jada."

I looked up at Tryst, who nodded.

"Okay," I said, leaning closer to B so I could rest my head against hers. "You're gonna be okay, girl. I promise." I eased away once she was out, and watched as a pickup hauled a flatbed trailer carrying four cowboys, including Tex, close to us. Three more men jumped out of the truck's cab. They rolled the horse onto a stretcher bigger than any I'd ever seen, then the twelve of them hefted it onto the flatbed.

"I want to go with her!" I shouted.

"Go ahead," Zin said. "I'll take care of your horse."

"B is my horse," I said, climbing onto the flatbed and sitting down beside her. On the bumpy ride to the barn, I stroked her neck. I could see bite marks there and on other places on her body. "They attacked her," I cried.

Tex put his arm around my shoulder. "She's gonna be okay, Jada. We'll all take real good care of her."

Tears streamed down my cheeks. "She was so afraid."

"She's safe now." Tex rubbed her belly. "She's gonna be okay, and soon, the two of you will be back out on the trail."

I appreciated his words, but I knew differently. It would take time for B's leg to heal, and until the vet was able to determine how bad the break was, it would be impossible to predict how long. Even then, would she ever feel safe enough to ride out on the trails again?

"Someone needs to stay with her twenty-four/seven to make sure she doesn't come to and try to stand," said the vet as he was getting ready to leave. "I'll be back in an hour or two with the portable X-ray, then we'll determine our next course of action."

"She's not going to be put down," I blurted.

I felt a hand on my shoulder and looked up at Tryst. "If that's what is best for her, that is what we will do. We cannot allow Berta to endlessly suffer, little one."

I shook my head. "You'll have to get through me to do it, and I'm not leaving her side. I'll eat and sleep here until she's fully recovered."

No one spoke other than the vet, who said he'd return as soon as he could.

I didn't pay attention to who stayed or left. I kept my focus solely on B until I felt Zin enter the stall. I didn't have to look. I knew it was him.

"Hey," he said, sitting beside me. He stroked B's belly like Tex had on the ride here. Neither of us spoke again until he put one arm around my shoulders and I leaned into him.

"I won't let them kill her," I said, burying my face in his neck. "She's hurt. That doesn't mean she has to die. It just means she has to be given what she needs to get better." I looked up when I felt Zin's body shudder and saw his tears.

"That's right, baby. She just has to be given what she needs."

I had no idea what time it was when the vet returned and asked Zin and me to step out of the stall so he could X-ray B's leg.

"I'll leave, but I'm going to watch," I warned him.

"You need to step farther away," Tryst said, holding out his hand. "The doctor is only going to get the X-ray. I swear that to you."

I looked into his eyes and let him lead me out of the barn. I glanced over my shoulder, relieved when I saw Zin right behind us.

There were so many questions I wanted to ask. What was he doing here? How long had he been on the ranch?

The hardest question I needed to ask was of Tryst. "Excuse us," I said, looking behind me a second time. Once he and I were far enough away that we could speak privately, I stopped. "Did you know he was here?"

"Not until earlier, when he and Brix showed up in the pasture. When you asked, I didn't know he'd come with my nephew. I would not lie to you, Jada."

I studied him. Tryst *wouldn't* lie. I knew that in my heart. "I'm sorry."

He cupped my cheek. "Don't be."

"I know you're an honest man, Tryst. I shouldn't have questioned you."

"There is nothing wrong with asking for reassurance."

"What about B? What do you think will happen?"

"I cannot answer you truthfully until we know the X-ray results."

The vet came out of the barn, walked over to his vehicle, and took a bag out of the passenger seat, then he pulled a laptop out of the bag. He came over to where Tryst and I stood. "Ready to take a look?" he asked.

I followed the doctor, and Tryst followed me with his hand on the small of my back.

"Would you mind if Zin joined us?" I asked when we got closer to where he waited. While it might not be fair, considering the circumstances, I didn't care right now. If the news was bad, I wanted him with me.

"Not at all." Tryst motioned for Zin to follow us inside.

The vet set his laptop on the desk and inserted a flash drive. Seconds later, the image loaded on the screen. "As you can see, the break is here, but it's not as bad as I anticipated. It's actually more of a fracture. We'll need to do everything possible to keep her weight off it so it doesn't get worse. I can get a cast on it now. That will help."

After the vet finished putting on the cast and left, Zin and I returned to B's stall, where someone had laid out several blankets. There were also two low folding chairs in the corner. "She's such a great horse," I said, sitting down next to her.

"I saw you with her." His eyes were wide when they met mine.

"It *was* you I saw."

He nodded. Zin was rarely at a loss for words, but I'd come to learn the look he got on his face when he was. His upper lip tightened and quivered just a little. Hardly noticeable unless you were paying attention, and I was.

"Did you arrive on Friday?"

He nodded a second time.

"I could feel you here. I thought I was losing my mind, especially after Tryst assured me you weren't on the ranch. I mean, you were with Brix."

"We've been working on his house."

I hated how tentative he was being with me, but could it be helped? I'd ordered him away, told him I didn't want to see him, never responded to his texts.

"Zin?"

He'd looked away, but returned his gaze to mine.

"I know this is a lot to ask. I also know it isn't fair, but would you hold me?"

16

Zin

A lot to ask? Unfair? God, it's what I'd been dreaming about, praying for. I scooted closer and opened my arms. Jada turned sideways and rested against me, then pushed me down on the blanket. I felt like the biggest asshole alive when my cock stiffened. This was about comfort. Not sex. Jada turned so her back was to my front, and we both faced her horse.

From what Bones had said, there were whip wounds only on her chest. There weren't any on her back. While I'd wrapped her in a blanket and carried her in my arms from the radio station, all I'd cared about at the time was getting her the hell out of there. I hadn't looked her over before I did so.

I kept my arms loose around her, not wanting to cause any pain. When she put her hands on my arms to tighten my hold, I almost wept with relief.

There were so many things I wanted to say, but none I was brave enough to. According to the messaging app, she'd read both my texts. The first, saying I missed her so fucking much I couldn't breathe. The second, saying I loved her. She hadn't replied, which might mean she didn't know what to say.

After I'd sent the second one, part of me wished I could recall it. Now, I was glad I hadn't. Whether she wanted to or not, I was just enough of a selfish bastard that I needed her to know.

I closed my eyes and breathed in her scent, so thankful I could. That this wasn't a dream. When I heard her breathing even out, I knew she'd fallen asleep. I wouldn't, though. One of us had to stay awake to keep an eye on Berta. If Jada needed me to do it, I'd stay awake twenty-four hours a day.

The words she'd spoken replayed in my head. "She's hurt. That doesn't mean she has to die. It just means she has to be given what she needs to get better."

When I'd responded almost verbatim, agreeing with her, I wasn't talking about the horse. Did Jada realize how close to home those words hit?

A chill went through me. One sentence. *That doesn't mean she has to die.* Jesus, was that how Jada felt? Had she considered taking her own life? Did she think she wasn't worthy of going on living? I prayed not. I prayed it was just a reaction to believing the horse was about to be euthanized.

The sun had barely set when Tryst came into the stall. Jada's eyes opened immediately, as though she'd sensed his arrival.

"Take a break," he said to her.

Jada shook her head. "I'm okay. I can stay."

While I'd seen Tryst angry at things that happened, or even people who'd committed crimes or wronged others, I couldn't say I'd ever seen him mad at someone he was close to. Especially not Jada. "I told you to take a break."

From the corner of my eye, I could see her shock at his tone.

When she asked him what was wrong, I couldn't help but wonder if his anger was directed at me for being there with her. I removed my arm that was around her and stood, holding my hand out to her, but she shook her head. "I'm not leaving."

Tryst crouched down in front of her. "You are putting your recovery at risk. You aren't managing your pain. You haven't eaten since last night, and then you hardly touched your food. I cannot allow you to do these things, little one."

I wanted to belt him when her cheeks turned pink and her eyes filled with tears. I understood his concern. It was the delivery I had a problem with.

"I'll take you to the house," I offered.

Jada stood without taking my outstretched hand. "Would you excuse us?"

It took me a second to realize she was talking to me. "Um, sure." I wanted to stay close enough to eavesdrop, but things were tentative enough between us. I didn't want to give her another reason to push me away. I walked outside and looked up at the moon.

It was the same one I'd looked at every night since arriving with Brix and Addy, yet the chill it gave me every other night didn't feel quite as cold. It was so clear that I could see millions of stars, but none that shot across the sky. Maybe because I'd gotten my wish. At least part of it. I was here. I'd held Jada in my arms because she asked me to. For now, that was enough.

I was stunned when Tryst walked out of the barn instead of Jada.

"Stubborn," he muttered, shaking his head.

"Do you think you were a little hard on her?"

"Perhaps." He joined me where I stood, leaning against the corral's fence. "I didn't know how else to get through to her. Not that it worked."

I wondered why he hadn't started off with a softer approach, but I wasn't privy to their conversations over the last few days. Maybe he already had.

"I hope you're not angry I'm here, Tryst."

"Part of me suspected you were, especially since Jada felt your presence so strongly."

"If it hadn't been for the horse, I never would've—"

He raised his hand. "It evolved the way it was supposed to. Jada could only lower her walls and accept your comfort because it was about something—someone—other than herself."

"I'm glad you feel that way."

He nodded, but his eyes were tight.

"You're worried."

"Jada is not as lost as she believes she is. However, she is far more withdrawn than you realize. Do not allow yourself false hope, Vaile."

I didn't want to hear him say what I already knew. Nothing would be as simple as me showing up here right when she needed me the most and Jada and I reconciling. If that's what we were doing. I had no idea. Why? Because she and I didn't talk about stuff like this. Important shit. We fucked, we laughed, we teased each other, then we fucked some more. Yeah, I'd told her I loved her, but that didn't mean I knew how to be the person she needed or wanted in her life. She hadn't talked about it either. We hadn't talked about anything. Not in four fucking years, and both of us were equally to blame.

Could we change? Could we start communicating, or were we too settled into the way things were?

"How did you leave things with her?" I asked.

"I have agreed to ask the nurse to bring medication to the barn. In exchange, Jada has agreed to eat the food Lynne also brings."

I chuckled. "Doesn't sound like much of a win on your side."

Tryst shook his head. "Jada isn't my niece by blood, but I've always considered her to be. As I reminded her, she called me Uncle Tryst until she decided she was too old for such things. Anything that helps her heal, I will consider a win."

"I feel the same way."

Tryst put his hand on my shoulder. "I know you do."

"Don't even think about it," Jada said to me when I walked into the stall.

I held up both hands. "Whatever you think I'm about to say or do, I'm not."

"I'm not leaving her."

I sat beside her on the blanket. "I know you're not, and guess what? I'm not leaving you."

"You don't have to stay, Zin."

"But will you let me if I really, really want to?"

She smiled. "I've never been able to say no to you, have I?"

Not until very recently, but I had no intention of reminding her of that now.

Lynne came to the barn with more food than the two of us could eat, but when it came time to take her meds, Jada was reluctant. "Just ibuprofen," she insisted. "I don't want to be groggy if B needs me."

The nurse's eyes met mine. After I told her I'd be here in case anything "went south," the nurse left.

"Went south? What's that mean?" said Jada, poking me once Lynne was gone. "You're such a dweeb."

I reached out to tickle her, like I did whenever she teased me, but I pulled back.

Jada's eyes darkened. "What was that?"

"I didn't want to, you know, hurt you."

"You didn't want to hurt me, or you don't want to touch me?"

"What? That's ridiculous. Of course I want to touch you."

"I don't believe you." She folded her arms, then dropped them as if their pressure hurt.

"If I could, I'd have my hands on you every minute of the day. You're the one always slapping me away."

"That was…before."

I shook my head enough for it to feel like my teeth rattled. "Wrong. Do you know how hard it's been for me not to kiss you? God, Jada, I want you so bad I feel like I'm going to explode."

"You should go."

"What the hell just happened? I should go because I was afraid it would hurt if I tickled you? You can't be serious."

Her glare told me that was the last thing I should've said. I seemed to be on a roll.

"Leave, Zin."

When she was at Butler Ranch, I'd respected her wishes. No more. "I'm not going anywhere."

She stood, so I did too. "Get out!" she shouted, pushing me toward the stall's entrance.

I stood my ground. "What the fuck, Jada? Stop this. I didn't say or do anything to cause this reaction from you."

"What did you think would happen if you touched me? Would it burn your fingers? Would you find me so repulsive that you had to run from the barn before you lost your dinner?" She pushed me again. This time, my back hit the stall's wall.

"I'll say it one more time." I raised my voice. "I didn't tickle you, because I was afraid I'd hurt you. There's never been a time in my life I haven't wanted to touch you." I shook my head. "It was all I could do to keep my hands off you even when I knew you were too young for me to act on my attraction."

"Bullshit." She sneered at me.

"Don't do this," I pleaded. "Don't push me away again."

When she threw herself at me, I wanted to keep her body from touching mine, knowing how much it would hurt when it did. I stopped myself, though, knowing that if I did, she'd take it as another indication I didn't want her.

She grabbed the front of my shirt and slammed her lips against mine. Then she thrust her tongue into my mouth and pressed until our teeth ground. No matter how much I tried to slow things down, Jada's assault on me—and that's exactly what it was—continued.

The next thing I knew, she pulled me away from the wall and pushed me hard enough for me to stumble and fall on the blankets. She walked over and put her boot on my thigh, making me want to protect my cock if she decided to move her foot to the left.

I lay there, watching as she removed her foot from where it rested on my leg, unfastened her jeans, and pushed them down her legs. She toed off her boots and stepped the rest of the way out of her pants.

There was never a time when I didn't fantasize about Jada's naked pussy, sometimes even when she was in bed beside me and I wasn't touching it. I was hard as steel, straining against my fly, but this felt all wrong, especially when she spread my legs, knelt between my thighs, and unfastened my belt, then my jeans. She reached in and freed my cock, then straddled me, rubbing it back and forth through her wetness.

I put my hands on her legs. "Jada, slow down."

"Slow down or stop? Which is it, Zin? You want me so bad you're gonna explode, or the thought of being inside me repulses you."

With a growl, I grabbed her waist and thrust all the way into her. If that was what she wanted, that was what she was going to get, but I'd be damned if I let her control it.

I rolled us both until she was on her back, grabbed both her ankles, and raised them so they rested against my chest and shoulders. This was Jada's favorite position. The one that never failed to make her come.

"You thought I didn't want to touch you? Didn't want you? Wrong, Jada. I will always want you.

Always. A hundred years from now, I'll still fuck you whenever you let me. Every day."

Her neck arched, and the look on her face was one I knew well. Intimately. "Come on, Jada. Give me another one." I let her legs drop, put my hands under her ass, and jackhammered into her.

Two things happened at once. I heard the barn door open and footsteps headed our way. At the same time, I saw tears rolling down Jada's cheeks. I pulled out and was grabbing a blanket to cover her when I heard a roar, then felt myself being lifted by the back of my shirt. Whoever had a hold of me slammed me into the wall. The air left my body, and I struggled to breathe, only to have him slam me against it a second time.

"Montano, stop!" Jada screamed as he did it a third time, hard enough that I saw stars. Suddenly, he was off me. I spun around and saw Press had Onyx in a neck hold.

"Get out of here!" Press yelled.

I shook my head and looked down at Jada. She was sobbing.

"I can't hold him much longer. Get the fuck out of here, Zin," Press repeated.

My eyes met hers. "Go," she whispered before turning away from me.

"What's goin' on in here?" I heard another voice shout.

"Get Zin out of the barn," Press ordered. "Now!"

I stumbled out of the stall and came close to face-planting, but I reached out to grab something to keep me upright. It was an arm, and I had a death grip on it.

"Help me," the man I recognized as Tex said to a second guy. With one on each side of me, they got me out of the barn and into the open door of a truck.

17

Jada

My brother knelt in front of me. "I will fucking kill him," he seethed, covering me with one of the blankets. "I'll rip him to pieces with my bare hands."

"What are you talking about?" I shouted at him.

"He *raped* you!"

"God, Montano, have you lost your mind?"

"I saw him. I saw what he was doing to you."

I sat up and winced when the adrenaline had worn off enough that the searing pain in my chest flared. "We were having sex. He didn't rape me."

"I know what I saw. That wasn't sex. That was violent and ugly. That was *assault*," he yelled.

I glared at him. "You know nothing about Zin and me. That's how we fuck, Montano. It gets us both off, asshole," I shouted back at him. "We've been doing it for years, bro." I emphasized every word, and my eyes bored into his, daring him to challenge me. He fell backwards and leaned against the wall.

"You and Zin?"

I stood and got in his face. "Yeah, me and Zin. You got a fucking problem with that?"

"I didn't…is that why…" He put his head in his hands.

"Spit it out, Montano. Is that why he was there? Why he shot and killed Al Zaabi? Why he risked his own life to save mine?"

"No one told me."

I sat down in front of him. "Because no one knew."

He raised his head. Fired burned in his eyes like it had when he barged in and pulled Zin off me. "How long?"

"None of your goddamn business."

"How long, Jada?" he shouted.

"Four years, asshole. We've been fucking for four years."

"Don't talk like that."

I shook my head. "I'm not a kid, Montano. I'm a grown woman."

"Do you love him?"

I shrugged. I did, but there was no way in hell I'd admit it to my brother before I told Zin. "I care about him."

"What about him? How does he feel?"

The message Zin had sent said he loved me, but we hadn't talked about it. Until we did, what was between us was no one else's business. "I'm not sure," I said when he repeated the question.

We sat in silence for several minutes. I was the first to speak. "You gotta quit beating up my boyfriend, bro."

He smiled, but it didn't stay on his face long. "You were crying. Did he hurt you?"

I shook my head. "Not as much as I hurt him," I said under my breath.

Montano called Tryst and asked if he could have someone come to the barn to stay with Berta after I'd explained why I couldn't leave her. When Tex and another cowboy showed up, I let my brother take me back to Tryst's place. Zin wasn't there, not that I expected him to be. I went into the bedroom and called, but it went straight to voicemail.

I stuck my head out the door and motioned to Lynne, who came in and shut it behind her.

"Are you okay?" she asked, pulling a piece of straw from my hair.

I took it from her hand. "I'm fine. Have you heard anyone say anything about Zin?"

Her eyes darkened. "They took him to the hospital."

I grabbed her wrist. "Where? I mean which hospital?"

"I think there's only one."

I rushed out of the room to where Tryst sat talking with Montano. "Where is Zin?" I demanded.

Both men looked at me with blank stares.

"Don't pretend like you don't know. Lynne just told me you took him to the hospital."

Tryst's eyes were wide.

"I didn't say he did. One of the cowboys swung by here, looking for him." She looked at Tryst. "You, I mean."

"I just returned." He had an odd look on his face, as if he didn't want to divulge where he'd been.

"Can you find out which hospital?"

Tryst stood. "There is only one. I will take you."

"You, stay here," I told my brother when he stood. "You've done enough." Something occurred to me. "How did you know Zin was here?"

He shook his head. "I didn't. I came to see you."

"Wasn't Press with you?"

"He offered to fly down with me."

Something about the way he'd phrased his statement made me think he was leaving something out.

However, I couldn't worry about that now. "When I get back, you and I are going to talk."

Montano smiled. "You know it, sis. You've got a lot of explaining left to do."

Like hell, I did, I thought, following Tryst out to the truck.

"What happened?" he asked once we were on the road.

"Montano caught us, uh, fooling around."

Tryst's eyebrow shot up.

"Come on, I've been seeing him for four years. You couldn't have thought I meant anything other than having sex."

He smiled and shook his head.

"I'm a grown woman," I said to him like I had to my brother.

"You will not get any argument from me. And just so you know, I'm happy to hear you were, uh, fooling around."

I half smiled and looked out the passenger window. He wouldn't feel that way if he knew how it had come about. It wasn't the first time Zin and I had had "angry sex," but it had pushed the limits of what it could be considered.

When we pulled up to the hospital, Zin and Press were walking out the main entrance doors. I got out of the truck and rushed over to him. "Are you okay?"

He nodded and motioned to his bandaged nose. "Broken for sure this time. At least, it was from hitting the wall, not from your brother's fist."

"I'm sorry."

I expected Zin to say something in response to my apology, but he didn't.

"Will you excuse us?" I said to Tryst. "Uh, hi, Press."

He raised a hand. "Hi, Jada."

When I walked away, Zin followed.

"I'm sorry," I repeated once we were several yards from them.

"What for?"

I bit my lip. "Everything?"

He shook his head and started to leave, but I grabbed his arm.

"Don't go. We need to talk."

He spun around and stepped closer. "Are we gonna do that, Jada? Are we gonna talk? Cuz I feel like we never do."

I nodded. "Yes. We're going to talk. We need to."

He looked up at the sky, then down at me. "I saw a shooting star the night you left to come down here."

"Did you make a wish?"

He shook his head. "I didn't know which one to make." He took another step, so close I could feel his breath. "You see, I had two. The first was for you to get better"—he paused and took a deep breath—"regardless of whether I was part of your life or not. The second was that you'd let me help you."

I shivered. "Let's talk."

"Where? Here, in the hospital parking lot?"

I couldn't tell if he was joking. However, given his mood, I guessed he wasn't.

"Hey, Tryst? Are any of the *casitas* you mentioned when I arrived available?"

"Many are."

"We just need one."

"We'll follow you," Zin said, getting into the car with Press.

"Can I give you some uncley advice?" Tryst asked after we'd been driving a few minutes.

"Sure."

He hesitated and looked away. Two things very un-Tryst-like. "I speak from experience, little one. Be honest. Tell Zin how you truly feel. Do not make the mistakes I have. Do not lose this chance for love."

"Mistakes with Rosa?" I asked.

"No." His white-knuckle grip on the steering wheel, combined with the curtness of his response, made it clear the topic was not open for further discussion.

When we pulled into the ranch's driveway, Press kept going on the road.

Tryst reached over and put his hand on mine. "Give it time. I'm sure he'll come to the house."

The fifteen minutes I waited for him to arrive felt longer than an hour. I'd broken myself of the habit of chewing my fingernails when I was a teenager, but now, they were bitten to the point of almost bleeding.

The first thing I'd done when we returned was tell my brother to leave. Tryst offered him the use of a *casita*, but he said he'd stay at Brix's place. When Press' vehicle pulled up, Montano went out at the same time Zin came inside.

"I needed to pick up some stuff," he explained, raising a duffel bag.

"Ready?" Tryst asked, carrying my bag over. "We're going to the closest of the *casitas,* in case you need the nurse for anything," he said, leading us a few yards from the main house.

When he unlocked the door and opened it, I saw someone had lit the fireplace.

"I asked one of the guys to get the place warmed up," he said, not stepping more than a few feet inside. "The refrigerator and pantry are stocked with food and beverages. If you need anything else, send me a message, and I'll either bring it over myself or have it delivered."

"Thank you, Tryst." I leaned up and kissed his cheek.

"Remember what I said."

I nodded. "Thanks again."

He closed the door behind him, leaving Zin and me alone.

"What did he say?"

I walked over and sat near the fire, warming my hands. "He said to be honest and tell you how I feel."

"Will you?"

I nodded.

"No, Jada. I need to hear the words. Will you tell me how you feel?"

"Yes, Zin."

He dropped the bag he still held in his hand to the floor. "Then, I'll stay."

I walked down the hallway and saw there was only one bedroom.

"I can sleep on the sofa if it would make you more comfortable," he offered. His eyes bored into mine as if he was challenging me to ask if that meant he didn't want me.

"It wouldn't make me feel more comfortable."

He nodded and brought both our bags into the room. I turned on the light and saw there were meds on the dresser. Tryst must've asked Lynne to leave them at the *casita*.

"When do you need to take these?" Zin asked, picking up one of the bottles.

"I'm trying to wean myself from them, but I take them when I feel the pain getting worse." I studied his face. "It looks like you need them more than me. How bad does it hurt?"

Zin shook his head. "What really hurts is my pride, and I doubt your medicine will ease that pain."

I touched his cheek. "He thought you were raping me."

He jerked away and stalked out of the bedroom. I followed.

"I told him you weren't. I also told him we'd been seeing each other for a few years."

Zin was standing in front of the fireplace, his hand on the mantle. When he dropped his head to his chest, I approached and put my hand on his shoulder.

"Will you tell me how you feel?" He repeated.

I'd said I would, but I needed him to do the same.

I lowered my hand and walked away, and he spun around to face me. "Why was it a secret for so long, Jada? Why did it take your brother thinking I was raping you for you to admit what's between us?"

"That's not fair. You didn't want anyone to know, either."

"Why? I don't understand why we both felt like we had to keep it a secret."

I sat on the hearth, and Zin sat beside me, close enough for me to put my head on his shoulder. "In the beginning, I think it was because we didn't know how to define it. Actually, I think that's always been the case. Even recently before…you know."

"How do we define it?"

I pondered his question for several seconds. Prior to Al Zaabi holding me captive and torturing me, I probably would've said something trite like we were boyfriend and girlfriend. It wasn't that simple anymore. The Jada Zin had known on New Year's Day no longer existed. What happened to me had irrevocably changed me physically, mentally, and emotionally. "I don't know," I finally whispered.

I felt Zin's body tighten. I knew my words hurt him, but what I'd agreed to was telling him how I felt. I couldn't reassure him by lying. It wouldn't do either of us any good.

"Do you want me here?"

It would be so easy, so simple, to say I did. But what he was truly asking of me terrified me. "Do you want to be here?" I asked instead.

Zin stood and paced the room. "Is it really so fucking hard for you to say it? If you *don't*, say it. If you *do*, say it."

I lowered my head and let my tears fall freely. "Is it so hard for you to accept that I don't know who I am anymore? That my life has changed, and it will never go back to the way it was?"

He cocked his head. "Why not? People heal, Jada. It takes work. It's hard. It's painful. But they process through their trauma and recover from it."

"Not always." I thought about my brother. Montano was a pilot. It was his passion, and he'd never wanted to be anything else. He first flew fighter jets in the military. After he came out of the coma following the plane crash, the doctors told him he'd never pilot again. Would he ever truly recover from it? I didn't have any idea, because it wasn't the kind of thing he and I discussed.

It was the same with Luisa. Like me, had she lost her ability to live without fear? Again, I didn't know. I'd been her friend. I'd been with her. But I hadn't been brave enough to ask the tough questions. The kind Zin was asking me.

"It's been a long, difficult, and very emotional day. Can we please talk in the morning?"

Zin nodded, but when I told him I was going to bed, he didn't join me.

18

Zin

Was it fair I was angry? Beyond it, really. My patience had run out, but maybe it was because, as she'd said, it had been a long, difficult, and very emotional day. My whole head throbbed, but the ache in my chest hurt far worse. I felt Jada slipping away. Physically felt it. Yet I wondered if there was anything I could do to prevent it.

I longed for her easy smile. Her laughter. Her sense of humor and adventure. The time we'd spent together had always been fun. Sure, we'd argued. Not about important stuff, though. Mainly, she gave me shit about the kind of law I practiced. Actually, she questioned my ethics. So I was wrong. If that wasn't important, nothing was.

It spoke to the kind of man I was. Or of the way she saw me. Who knew better? Her or me? Sometimes, it took looking at ourselves from another's perspective to get an accurate read on how we presented ourselves.

There wasn't time or a reason for me to tell her I'd decided to close my practice. I'd made the decision for myself, based on how I felt about my life. However, I worried Jada would be skeptical and think I was doing it because of her. Which meant she'd think I was lying about it. That in itself was an issue. Why would I lie? And worse, why would she think I was? Could a relationship survive if the two people involved didn't believe or trust each other?

Maybe the hurdles we faced were bigger than superficial. Maybe we were fundamentally unsuited to be together.

I sat in a chair and leaned forward, resting my elbows on my knees. I let my head fall forward, then sat straight up when the throbbing intensified.

Fucking Onyx. I had a problem with him too, and it ran deeper than him physically assaulting me. Did he really think I'd rape his sister? We'd known each other most of our lives. Never in a million years would I accuse him of such a thing. It wouldn't matter how angry I was about him "interfering in an op." I had saved his goddamn sister's life. He should be on his knees, thanking me, not slamming me against walls and accusing me of rape.

I stood and was on my way to the door, unsure whether, once I walked out, I'd clear my head in the fresh air and return inside or take the trail up to Brix's place and hop on a flight home tomorrow. I had my hand on the knob when I heard Jada's voice.

"Zin?"

"What?" I snapped, immediately wishing I hadn't. "Sorry," I muttered.

"Where are you going?" she asked.

"I haven't decided."

"Are you leaving?"

"Like I said."

My back was to her, so I wasn't expecting it when she approached and put her arms around my waist and rested her head against me. I felt the dampness of her tears on my shirt.

"Jada…"

"Yeah?"

"Please don't do anything to hurt yourself."

"Right now, nothing hurts worse than the chasm between us."

"Before I turn around, I want to make myself crystal clear."

I felt her nod. "Go ahead."

"Any hesitancy you feel on my part is *solely* out of fear of hurting you. *Nothing* else."

"Okay."

"Not just 'okay,' Jada. I need you to tell me you understand and accept I'm telling you the truth." If she couldn't, there was no point in sticking around.

"I understand."

I wanted more. More words. More reassurance. However, we weren't in a courtroom. I couldn't grill her like I would a witness.

"Come to bed," she pleaded.

"If I do, it will be to sleep. Nothing else is going to happen between us until we talk." I couldn't believe those words came out of my mouth. Nothing had changed. I still wanted her so badly I felt like my cock—more than my head—would explode. But I wanted to talk more. I wanted to know where I stood with her. If the time had come for us to end this, I didn't want to think back on tonight being our last fuck.

On the other hand, maybe we should have sex to replace the memory of what had happened between us in the barn.

She let go of my waist, took my hand, and led me into the bedroom. I hadn't turned around to look at her, so I hadn't known all she was wearing was a sweatshirt that looked several sizes too big and a pair of panties. "Nice sweatshirt," I commented.

She faced me. "Are you being sarcastic?"

"No. Jesus, Jada. It was an innocent fucking comment."

Her eyes scrunched like she was about to cry. "I took it from you a couple of years ago. I thought you were teasing me."

I groaned and looked up at the ceiling. If we had trouble joking around with each other, how in the hell were we going to tackle the big stuff?

"Zin, please. Let's just go to bed."

I went into the bathroom to take a quick shower. When I came out, Jada was softly snoring. I eased into bed, hoping I wouldn't wake her, and shut my eyes.

When the sun rose, I'd hardly slept. Every time Jada moved, I worried I'd somehow hurt her. My back ached from keeping myself as far over on the edge of the mattress as I could.

After rolling off the bed—as opposed to out of it—I went into the kitchen and made coffee before checking the fridge for something to eat.

"Good morning." Jada joined me, looking sexy as fuck in the same thing she wore last night.

"Mornin'." I poured a cup of coffee and handed it to her before getting my own.

"You didn't sleep." Jada had always been in tune with me, so her comment didn't surprise me.

"I didn't want to inadvertently hurt you." I held my breath, waiting for her to challenge me, and let it out when it didn't appear she would. "Do you want to go to the barn this morning?" I figured she'd want to check on Berta at least, maybe stay with her.

She sipped her coffee and leaned against the counter. "I thought you wanted to talk."

"The two things aren't mutually exclusive," I snapped, again wishing my tone didn't throw light on the anger sitting so close to the surface.

Jada didn't react. Instead, she walked over to the window. "It's so beautiful here, isn't it? Have you had much time to explore?"

I stood beside her. "Not on this trip, but I have in the past."

"Have you visited the temple?"

I shook my head. I wasn't big on religion or much to do with it, so I'd avoided it.

"It's worth it."

"Maybe I'll do that."

Jada turned so she faced me rather than the window. "This is different for us."

"Meaning?" This time, I did a better job of tempering my anger.

"We don't usually wake up and plan our day. I either leave, or we know we'll be in bed most of the time if I stay."

"We do more than have sex." I walked over and poured myself more coffee. When I held up the pot, she joined me and set her cup on the counter so I could refill it.

"Do you need to work on the house with Brix?"

I smiled. "I think that was more of a ruse to get me to Mexico."

"Tryst keeps an extra golf cart at the house for my use. I usually go to the meditation center first, then ride. Although I would like to check on B before anything else today."

"Would you like me to go with you?"

Jada glared at me, and rather than pissing me off, it made me weirdly happy.

"Why are you smiling?" she demanded.

"You're hot when you're irritated with me."

She smiled, too, and rolled her eyes. "This from the guy who said all he wanted to do was sleep."

"Look, I hate how awkward it is between us. It feels like it's ninety degrees outside, and I have a heavy winter coat sewn onto my body. I'm sure there's a way to get out of it, but I can't figure out how."

This time, Jada raised a brow. "First, I feel it too. Second, good analogy, Zin. What do we do?"

"I know I said I wanted to talk. Or maybe you said it first, but now, I think we should wait. Let's just *be* for today—maybe a couple of days—see if we can find our rhythm again."

The woman smirked. "Will sex stay off the table?"

My gut told me that was the right way to play this, but my cock was adamantly opposed. My brain didn't know which to listen to. While my gut was closer in proximity, my cock was much louder.

She bit her lip and responded before I did. "It might be best if we hold off for now."

"Jada, did—"

"No."

There was no doubt she knew what I'd been about to ask, and regardless of the fact both Doc and Bones assured me she hadn't been sexually assaulted, I needed her to confirm it. Saying all the words wasn't necessary. "There's something else I need to ask."

"I thought we weren't talking, Zin. Which is it? Are we, or aren't we?"

"We aren't." I left the kitchen and went into the bedroom. She followed.

"I'm sorry. Ask."

"Forget it." I was digging through my bag, not because I was looking for anything; I just didn't know what else to do.

Jada put her hand on my arm. "Sit down for a minute."

When I did, she sat beside me.

"There are countless ways this is hard for both of us. I know you, Zin. You want to fix it and make it all better. Me? I'd rather bury my head in the sand and forget it all happened. Neither of us can slide dealing with our shit into our comfort zone. Even if there weren't physical reminders, which there are, we have our own mental and emotional trauma to deal with. I can't take yours on, and you can't take mine on."

Her pain, her trauma was so much worse than mine. Why couldn't I take hers on? "I'm okay, Jada. I'm worried about you. I want to help you."

She took a deep breath. "Before Al Zaabi, had you ever killed someone?"

I shook my head when I feared I would choke up if I tried to speak.

"You don't think that was traumatic?"

"Why…" I shook my head a second time. As much as I wanted to understand, my reasons were selfish.

"Whatever it is, just ask."

It didn't matter how much it throbbed; I put my head in my hands. "That first day, at Butler Ranch, when I asked you what I did, why you wanted me to leave, the way you looked at me…" I couldn't go on.

"I told you to leave because you killed him."

"Why?"

She shrugged. "I wished I'd been able to do it. Exact my own revenge. Watch him pay. Watch him suffer, the way I did."

"I took that away from you."

"Maybe so, but you saved my life. I get that. If you hadn't shot him, I wouldn't be here. At least, I know he paid for what he did. I was there to witness it."

I looked up at her. "I wish there'd been another way."

Jada raised her chin and squared her shoulders. "There wasn't."

I stared down at the floor, afraid to ask the next question, but knowing I had to. "Jada, do you want to be in a relationship with me?"

Her eyes darted back and forth between mine. I held my breath, waiting for her reply until I couldn't any longer.

"Jada, please…"

Her eyes filled with tears, something I couldn't remember seeing before she was abducted.

She took a deep breath and let it out slowly. Even that sounded shaky. "I don't know."

19

Those three words were among the hardest I'd said in my life, but they were the truth. I didn't know if a relationship between Zin and me would work, whether I wanted it or not. I wasn't the same person as I had been a month ago. No amount of healing would change that.

In all the years he and I were together, I'd kept my worries, my weaknesses, my fears, and my bad moods from him. If I was feeling shitty, I left. When I walked out, the last thing he saw was a smile, no matter how hard I was crying on the inside.

Maybe that was one of the reasons I hadn't pushed for our relationship to go public. As it was, I had a built-in excuse to leave. Back to reality. Back to real life—whenever I wanted to. If people knew about us, my escape hatch wouldn't be so readily available.

If he got to know the real me, would he still want me? Especially now. I couldn't hide my physical wounds like I might be able to hide my feelings. Eventually, he would see them. Then what? Would he reject me? I wouldn't be able to handle it. Walking away from him permanently would hurt like a *sonuvabitch*. Him walking away from me would hurt worse than the lashes from Al Zaabi's whip.

Zin didn't move other than to turn away from me and look down at the floor. I knew that, at any second, he'd get up and walk out. He might catch the next flight to the States, and maybe it would be weeks or months before I saw him again.

My chest ached but not superficially. Deep inside.

"Should we go see Berta now?" he asked, glancing over at me.

"Wait. What? I just told you I didn't know if I wanted to be in a relationship with you."

He nodded. "I heard you."

I shook my head. "But—"

"Did you expect me to get pissed and leave?"

My eyes scrunched. "Honestly? Yes."

"If you'd said no instead of I don't know, I might've left. Not because I was pissed. Well, maybe a little, but more because I'd feel like my heart was being ripped out of my chest."

His words took all the air out of me. I was stunned speechless.

He stood and held his hand out. "Come on, *little one*. Let's go see your horse."

When I stood, I leaned up and kissed his cheek. I was incapable of more than that for now, even forming words.

Once outside, I tossed Zin the key to the golf cart. I was happy to let him drive. Trying to turn the damn thing pulled muscles that hurt like hell.

"I'd feel like my heart was being ripped out of my chest." Zin's words played over in my head. I studied his profile. Even with the skin around his nose black and blue, the man was hot as fuck. There were no better words to describe him.

He kept his dark-brown hair cut short, although right now, it had grown out enough that there was a little curl behind his ear. Some people looked good from the front or had a better side. Not Zin. Whether I was looking at him square in the face or at his profile, he was drop-dead good-looking. He had high cheekbones, and though his nose was broken, besides the bruising and it being a little swollen, it still looked perfectly shaped. And those lips? They'd brought such pleasure to every inch of my body. I squeezed my thighs together, thinking about the last time they had. Thinking about the last time his body, hard as chiseled stone, every muscle defined, had rested on mine. There was no better feeling in the world than Zin being inside of me.

"Hmm," I heard Zin mumble and turned to look at him. His eyes went from mine, down my body, and back again.

"What?" It was the first word I'd said since his heart comment.

He shook his head, smiled, and laughed. "You know I know what you're thinking about."

I folded my arms in an effort to hide my pointy nipples, but putting pressure on that part of my body still hurt.

Neither of us spoke again until we reached the barn, and then it wasn't to each other.

"Hey, Tex. How's Berta this morning?" I asked when we walked inside and saw him standing near her stall.

"Her ears perked up when she heard your voice."

"She's awake?" Zin asked.

"Still groggy. I've been with her all night, and she hasn't tried to stand. You better get in here before she does, though."

I brushed past him and knelt down beside her. "Hey, B," I said, soothing her. It wasn't strong or loud, but I was close enough to hear her nicker.

Zin came in and held up a face brush.

"You do it," I said rather than take it from him.

He knelt down on the other side of her and gently brushed her nose and head, then ran smooth strokes over the rest of her body. B's eyes fluttered closed, then opened again when he stopped. She neighed. He chuckled and kept going. When he got to her hind leg, he handed the brush to me, and I worked on her opposite side.

A few minutes later, Tryst arrived and poked his head in the stall. "The vet is here."

I nodded and eased away from B, who appeared to be sound asleep.

"You remind me of my Rosa…" Tryst looked over my head, and his eyes scrunched. I glanced around him, trying to place the woman walking toward us. "Jaicon," Tryst said, nodding once.

"Tryst," she responded.

"Have you met Jada Yáñez?" Tryst turned to me.

"You were Luisa's bodyguard…err…or something."

The woman smiled. "Close enough. How are you?"

"Good, thanks," I responded. I didn't know the woman, and even if I did, I couldn't tell her how often I'd held my breath, knowing my insides were like a pane of shattered glass, barely held together. If I allowed it to break apart, the pain would be unimaginable.

"Zin," she said, hardly glancing at him.

He nodded like Tryst had. Something was going on here, and while I was curious, my instincts told me to stay out of it.

"I can take over once the vet is finished if you would like to visit the meditation center," Tryst offered.

Zin and I left after I'd thanked him. Once we were out of the barn and closer to the golf cart, I brought up how strange the interaction with Jaicon had been. He raked his hand through his hair.

"She was in charge of your rescue mission, Jada."

"Oh." I walked around the cart and sat on the bench seat. "That explains her reaction to you, but what's up between her and Tryst?" Something else dawned on me. "What is she doing here?"

Zin sat beside me behind the wheel. "This hasn't been confirmed, but I think she and Tryst might be, uh, seeing each other."

"She's my age," I gasped.

Zin shook his head. "Luisa thought the same thing, but Jaicon said she's several years older."

"Several? No way." I tapped my cheek. "And how awkward was it that he just said Rosa's name?"

Zin shrugged. "So, where's the meditation center?"

I pointed toward the ridge where I'd seen someone standing, not knowing then it was him. "Head that way. It'll take us right to it."

"Is that the temple?" he asked, pointing west once we were halfway to our destination.

"It is. Do you want to go there first?"

"Nah. We don't have to."

"C'mon, let's."

Zin raked his hand through his hair a second time. It wasn't something I remembered seeing him do before.

"Do you need a haircut?"

He looked over at me. "Do I?" Before I could answer, he stared beyond me, kind of like Tryst had.

"What?" I asked, following his line of sight to where a lone coyote stood. It seemed like it was watching us.

"Shit," he said, shaking his head.

"I hate them," I said under my breath.

Zin nodded. "I felt the same way after they cost me a hundred grand in irrigation line."

"Tex said coyotes got into the pasture. That's what spooked B. We saw one on the trail too." I looked over to where we'd seen the animal a minute ago, but it was gone.

"Tomahawk told me they're sent to teach us something."

"Build fences they can't get through?"

He grinned. "There was one near the vineyards that I thought might be stalking me."

I remembered the dream I'd had and told Zin about it. "Tryst's reaction was the most interesting part. I woke with a start, and he asked what I saw. When I told him it was a coyote, he didn't say anything. He just nodded and smiled."

"Tommy said they visit in dreams too. His people believe they're spiritual beings."

I shook my head. "I find that hard to believe."

"He also told me to open my mind, and once I did, I'd recognize the lessons."

"I think he's stuck the thief in too many barrels without enough spitting."

Zin laughed out loud at my reference to the way winemakers tasted wine to see if it was ready to bottle. They rarely swallowed since they had to taste so much at one time. Instead, barrel rooms had grates in the floor, where they'd spit. "Maybe so, little one."

"What's with that?"

"What do you mean?" he asked, pulling up near the temple's entrance.

"Calling me 'little one.'"

He got out of the golf cart, came around to my side, and held out his hand. "I heard Tryst say it, and it seemed to fit."

It did from him, but not from Zin. "Don't, okay?"

He dropped my hand as if it had burned him. "Sure, yeah, not a problem."

"Come on. Don't get mad. It just seems weird."

He shrugged. "Like I said, not a problem."

"It's what my dad called me." He hadn't that I remembered, but I was trying to make a point.

Zin nodded. "Ew. Now I get it."

"See?"

He held my hand, and we walked to the temple's heavy wooden door. I'd come here almost every day since my first visit with Tryst. Like he had with me, I led Zin inside and to the center of the sanctuary, then told him to look up.

"Wow," he murmured, taking in the beauty of the skylights just like I had.

I took both his hands and turned them palms up. "Close your eyes and receive," I said, repeating Tryst's words, then walking away.

"Wait. Come back."

When I did, he put my right hand in his left so the back of it rested in his palm. Then he did the same with the opposite one.

"Let's receive together, Jada."

I closed my eyes and let the sun's rays wash over me, turning us both in a circle. When the warmth went away, I stopped.

"The first time I stood where we are now, I felt you. Tryst assured me you weren't here, but I knew you were. I told him about us."

"Yeah? What else did you tell him?"

I couldn't bring myself to confess that I told Tryst I needed to let Zin go. Nor could I tell Zin how we'd talked about why and the ways I'd changed both physically and emotionally. "He told me something."

"What?"

"That I called out for you in my sleep."

"What do you think that means?"

Rather than answer, I thought about how bright the sun was that day. "When we left, I looked up and thought I saw a man. I blinked, and it looked more like an animal. I blinked again, and they were both gone."

"What kind of animal?" he asked.

"A coyote."

We sat beside each other on one of the pews for so long I lost track of time. I hadn't answered when he asked what I thought calling out for him in my sleep meant, because I couldn't recall a time I'd even dreamed about him.

"How long are you staying?" I asked without looking at him.

"No timeline."

"What about work?"

He leaned back, wove his fingers together behind his head, and stretched his legs in front of him. "I'm retired."

"Right." I chuckled. Zin released his fingers and stretched his arm behind me, resting it on the back of the pew. I could feel his fingers in my hair and tried not to bristle. In the past, a simple touch, something like stroking my hair, running his finger down my cheek, kissing me—all of it had led to sex, and it had been explosive. Not angry, like it had been in the barn, more like the finale of a fireworks show.

I closed my eyes, trying to remember how him being inside me felt, like I had in the golf cart when I thought about his mouth. Now, I couldn't. As hard as I tried, I couldn't invoke how our two bodies fit together so perfectly it was as though we were puzzle pieces.

More, I couldn't feel him. He was sitting right next to me, and yet, it was as though my body had gone numb. That it had, worried me far more than what calling out for him in my sleep might mean.

Was that the reason the warmth under the steeple had gone away so quickly? Were the deities trying to tell us something?

20

Zin

"I wasn't joking about retiring," I said, waiting for her to react. She didn't. She appeared lost in thought, as though she hadn't heard me. "Jada?"

"What? Sorry."

"I said I wasn't joking—"

"I heard you."

Fuck. What the hell was going on now? Last night, I'd felt her slipping away, but then it had seemed like she wanted to work things out with me. Was she gone again? I hadn't liked roller-coasters much as a kid, and I liked them less now.

One minute, her hands were resting on mine and we were "closing our eyes and receiving" together. The next, she was as cold as when the sun hid behind a cloud and the warmth we'd been basking in from the steeple skylights went away. One minute, she's flirty, teasing me about being the one to say sex was off the table; the next, just my simple act of playing with her hair made her bristle.

"So, why?"

"Did I retire?"

She nodded.

I shrugged. "I didn't miss it."

Jada was looking straight ahead, not at me. "Maybe you'll change your mind."

I didn't respond since I couldn't tell if she was actually participating in our conversation or if her mind was elsewhere. Finally, she turned her head and looked at me.

"Sorry. I'm just not that into it, ya know?"

I did my best to keep myself from flipping out on her. "Not that into *what*?"

"Being a lawyer. It's why I didn't take the bar." Her eyes scrunched. "You're probably wondering why I wasted all that time and money on school."

"I'm not."

She raised a brow.

"I'm not lying. Why would I?"

She leaned back as if my words had slapped her. "I raised a brow, Zin. I didn't say you were lying."

"Why, then?"

"I don't know. I guess I feel guilty about it and worry you'll judge me."

I took my arm from behind her and leaned forward, resting my elbows on my knees. "I don't want to be that guy." I glanced over my shoulder, and she was studying me.

"You aren't, Zin."

I chuckled. "I remember plenty of times you said otherwise. What words did you use? Money-grubbing? All about the almighty dollar?"

"That was back when I was idealistic. Real life caught up with me."

I leaned back and put my arm around her, except this time, rather than play with her hair, I pulled her close to me. "There's nothing wrong with having ideals. Consider this—maybe you're rubbing off on me."

She rested her head against my chest. "I feel like I don't know myself anymore."

"You'll find your way back to who you've always been."

She stiffened.

I put my hand on her chin and raised it. "We all change and grow, baby. When I was a kid, I'd get chunky, then all of a sudden, it seemed like I grew two or three inches overnight and I was back to being a beanpole. It was still *my* body. It just needed time to adjust."

I knew she didn't buy my analogy when she scooted out of my arms, stood, and asked if I was ready to go to the mediation center.

We spent the next week trying to find our "rhythm." There were moments we connected and times I felt as though we didn't know each other at all. It was a byproduct of the kind of relationship we'd had for four years. It had been about sex, and now that we weren't having it, we had to figure out a way to be around each other.

After the first night, I'd wait until I was sure Jada was asleep, then I'd ease out of bed and sleep on the sofa. It's the only way my brain would allow my body to get any rest.

While I always got up before dawn and returned to bed, I knew Jada was aware I hadn't spent the night there, whether she acknowledged it or not.

"I got a message from Tryst, asking us to meet him at the barn," she said over our morning coffee.

"Did he say what about?"

She shook her head.

I set my coffee on the counter. "Let's go."

"Um, oh, okay."

I walked over and cupped her cheek. "You're worried. Let's find out what he wants to talk to you about."

She smiled and set her cup down too.

"Thanks for understanding," she said once we were in the golf cart. "You've been really great, Zin."

I'd been trying my damnedest. It wasn't just about attempting to anticipate the things she wanted to do and when she wanted to do them; it was being present when we did.

While Jada wasn't able to ride Berta, she took another horse, one Tryst eventually told us Jaicon planned to adopt. I used whatever horse Tex said needed exercise.

Before riding out, we spent an hour each day at the meditation center. I still doubted I was doing things right, but I sat beside her and mimicked her yoga poses the best I could.

There were other little things I did, like fill water bottles before we left for the day so we'd stay hydrated or light the candles at the center while she got out our mats.

When she was stiff at the end of the day, I'd rub her shoulders, keeping my touch light and as chaste as possible. Every once in a while, I'd kiss her cheek or she'd kiss mine, but that was as far as we went with our affection, other than holding hands.

Was my body happy about it? Hell, no. I still hadn't even seen her naked. I had no idea how bad the wounds on her chest were other than what I remembered seeing the day I'd carried her from the radio station wrapped in a blanket. I'd asked once if she needed my help with her bandages. She'd shut me down so fast that I didn't ask again.

Just the simple act of showering alone felt foreign to me. When she was at my place, we always showered together. Hell, half the time, we didn't make it through a single one without fucking.

I rolled my shoulders, reminding myself I'd rather be with Jada without sex than push her before she was ready and wind up losing her forever. My gut told me that was exactly what would happen.

Once at the barn, I parked and followed Jada inside. Tryst and the vet stood near the door to Berta's stall.

"What's wrong?" she asked, racing up to them.

"I did another X-ray. Her leg isn't healing as well as I'd hoped."

Jada started to shake. I put my arm around her, and she jerked away from me.

"She needs surgery, little one," Tryst told her, putting his hand on her shoulder. It stung when she didn't jerk it off.

"Surgery?" she repeated.

"That's right."

"Only surgery?"

"If you're asking if my intention is to euthanize her, the answer is no," said the vet. "However, there are risks inherent with every surgery. There's always the chance, no matter how minute, that she won't make it through."

My fists clenched at my sides when Tryst gathered her into his arms. I knew from the way her body shuddered that she was crying. Rather than stand there, wishing I was the one she'd turned to for comfort, I walked out of the barn. I leaned on the split-rail fence and watched as Tex worked with one of the horses. It was skittish, darting away from him whenever he got too close. At one point, it whinnied and reared. Tex got out of its way, rushing over, and standing by the fence about a foot away from me.

"What's the story with that one?" I asked.

"She was neglected and abused by an owner who had no goddamn idea what he was in for when he bought a green broke horse."

"How long has she been here?"

"About ten days. I've made progress with her, but some days, it feels like I take five steps back for every one I take forward." His gaze met mine. "Know what I mean?"

I doubted Tex was making a reference to Jada, but it sure felt the same to me. From the corner of my eye, I saw her walk out of the barn with Tryst, who still had his arm around her shoulders. I waited to see if she'd look for me or if she forgot I'd come to the barn with her.

The two stood and talked for a few minutes until Tryst motioned with his head in my direction. I wished he hadn't.

Jada leaned up, kissed his cheek, and walked over to me. "The vet is making arrangements to take Berta to the large animal hospital now."

"I'm sure sorry to hear that," Tex said before I could respond.

She thanked him, then turned to me. "So, um…"

I raised a brow, waiting for her to say whatever was on her mind. "I should probably see if Brix needs my help with anything," I finally said when I'd run out of patience.

Her eyes opened wide. "Are you angry about something?"

I glanced at Tex, who took the hint and walked away. I opened my mouth, but closed it. Could I tell her how much her actions hurt me? Would I sound like a total asshole if I reminded her how hard I'd been trying to be who and what she needed and that it felt like a slap in the face when she'd turned to Tryst for comfort instead of me?

"I'm not angry," I said instead.

"Seems like you are."

"Seems like you didn't need me back there, so I thought I'd make myself useful somewhere else."

Jada rolled her eyes and stalked away. I stayed where I was, wondering if she'd get in the golf cart and drive away, leaving me behind. She knew I'd left the key in it. I always did. Instead, when she got close, she turned around. "Are you coming?"

I didn't move. "Where you goin'?"

She put her hands on her hips and glared at me. "I don't know." When I still didn't move, she stalked over to me. "Dammit, Zin. I was sad, okay? And scared. I'm sorry I didn't stroke your fucking male ego and let you be the hero, but Tryst is…"

"Is what, Jada? Someone you trust more than me? Someone you believe wants the best for you more than I do? Cuz I'll tell you what, if I don't do it for you, say the word and I'll get out of your hair." I was taking this further than I'd intended to, acting like a damn kid, but she'd hurt me, and I was lashing out.

"I'm not interested in Tryst, if that's what you mean."

"No? Doesn't seem like you're all that interested in me either."

She raised her hand to slap me, but I grabbed her wrist. "I've had enough of you Yáñezes thinking you can haul off and hit me whenever you feel like it."

I let go of her wrist and took off toward the trail leading up to Brix's. I was bluffing before, but now I needed to pound a few nails into something hard.

21

Zin

When I got to the house and saw Onyx there, I realized how stupid it was for me to come here. He probably wanted to whale on me more than his sister did. Thankfully, Press got between the two of us, and Onyx went back to what he was doing.

"I was going to pay you a visit later," he'd said.

"Yeah? What for?"

"To tell you we're leaving tomorrow."

"I'm surprised you stuck around as long as you did."

"Yes, well…" He glanced at Onyx.

"I get it."

"How is Jada?" he asked, following me over to the ridge where I used to stand and hope for a glimpse of her.

"We had an argument."

"You and Jada? Say it isn't so!"

"Shut up, asshole."

"Her temper isn't any different than her brother's. I'm sure you know that better than the rest of us."

I shook my head. "It was my fault."

"Again, I'm stunned," he deadpanned.

"How's Luisa?" I asked in an attempt to change the subject.

"Worried about Jada."

"We all are. It's a day-by-day thing."

"It's good you're here. She needs you more than she realizes."

While that may have been true for Press and Luisa, I was beginning to think it wasn't for Jada and me. Maybe by turning to Tryst rather than me, she was trying to tell me something. "I'm not sure I'll stick around much longer."

"Leaving would be a mistake, Zin. One I'm sure you'll come to regret."

"Maybe." I looked back over at Onyx. "Are you in the middle of something?"

"Not particularly. Why do you ask?"

"Wanna go into town and get a beer?"

"There's little I'd like more, given I'm still here in Mexico. If I were home—"

"Rub it in, asshole."

One beer turned into two, then three. We stopped there and ordered food, and by the time we left the bar, Press had sobered up enough to drive and I'd had enough to see Jada.

Earlier—somewhere between my second and third drink—I'd admitted what led to the argument Jada and I had.

"Have you considered he's a father figure to her?" Press asked.

I thought about how I'd called her "little one" and she'd told me her dad used that name. "Yeah. I know he is."

"Before I say this, know you are my closest friend. There are times I feel closer to you than I do my brother. However, you can be intransigent—overly stubborn."

"I know what the word means, Press."

"I'm just saying that, right now, Jada needs you to focus solely on her. Set your own feelings aside for the time being."

"You don't think I have? Fuck, it's all I've done."

"And what you need to continue doing."

We returned to the ranch, and Press dropped me off at the *casita*. "Good luck, my friend," he said before I got out of the car.

"I have a feeling I'm going to need it."

"Groveling will become you."

I went inside, prepared to give Jada an apology. A big one. I just hoped she'd be willing to listen long enough for me to give it to her.

When I opened the door, she was sitting in the living room on the sofa, but she sprung to her feet. "Where were you?"

"I took the trail to Brix's place—"

"I know. Montano told me he saw you but you didn't stay long." She waved her hand in front of her face. "Are you *drunk*?"

"No, I'm not drunk. Fuck, Jada, I had a couple of beers with Press. He and your brother are leaving tomorrow."

"I know. Montano told me." She bit her lip. "Have you eaten?"

"Yeah, we got something in town."

"I was worried about you."

I wanted to tell her I worried about her every minute of every day, but I didn't come back here to argue. "I owe you an apology. I'm sorry I reacted the way I did earlier."

"Why did you?"

I shook my head. "To be honest, I don't know. Stupid male ego, like you said."

"I don't look at you and Tryst the same way."

"I know you don't."

"What you said about me not being interested in you. You're wrong about that too."

"I know." I rubbed my forehead. Maybe it was the beer or seeing Onyx again that had brought back the memory of being slammed up against the stall wall, but my head was pounding. Thinking about the stall reminded me of something. "How's Berta? Have you heard?"

"She pulled through. The vet said he used screws to reinforce her hind leg. When I left, she was still out from the anesthesia, but he said I could come back in the morning."

"You were there?"

"Tryst took me."

"Good. That's good." My headache was worsening. "Listen, I need to lie down. Can we talk more later?"

"Okay. Are you sure you're not hungry?"

I shook my head and went into the bedroom. It was early enough that I could sleep for a while, then get up once Jada came to bed and was asleep.

I drifted in and out of consciousness, dreaming Jada's lips were on my mine. When she deepened the kiss, I pulled her into my arms, groaning at how good it felt to hold her. She rubbed me through my jeans, and I moved her hand away to unfasten them, reaching in to free my rock-hard cock. God, I missed feeling her stroke me.

The dream was so vivid I felt on the verge of coming. When the tip of her tongue licked the slit, my eyes sprung open.

"Jada," I moaned when she took me into her mouth so deeply I felt her swallow on me. I ran my hands through her hair, wanting to pull her off me and push her to take me deeper equally. "What are you doing? If you don't stop right now—" She sucked harder, and I came. I pulled her body up beside me and stared into her eyes. "You didn't have to do that."

"I wanted to."

I leaned forward and kissed her like I'd longed to every minute of every day I'd been with her. She kissed me back, then pulled away. "I want you, Zin. I need you."

Her words alone got me hard again. "Are you sure?"

She nodded, reaching down to unfasten her pants.

"Let me, baby," I said, pushing her onto her back.

I took my jeans the rest of the way off, reached behind me, and pulled my shirt over my head, then took over as she shimmied her way out of her own jeans.

"I need these off too," I said, reaching underneath her butt to remove her panties. As I did, I looked into her eyes, but what I hoped to see, wasn't there. Jada wasn't there. I froze, staring at her. *Fuck. She didn't want this.* I felt sick to my stomach.

"You…why…" I cried. She was doing it because of what I'd said earlier. *"Goddammit, Jada!"* I shouted, rolling off her, off the bed. I grabbed my jeans and stalked out of the room.

"Zin!" she shouted after me. "Don't you fucking walk out on me, you bastard."

I heard her behind me and spun around just as she was about to slap me. I grabbed her wrist. "I told you earlier not to hit me!" I shouted just as her knee connected with my groin. "Jesus fucking Christ, what's wrong with you?" I seethed through gritted teeth as I cupped my throbbing cock.

"I hate you!" she screamed. "I fucking hate you." Jada didn't stop; she pummeled my arms, my back, anywhere she could connect with her fists.

"Stop it!" When I couldn't get a firm hold on her wrists, I wrapped my arms around her from the back and held hers to her sides. *"Settle down."*

She fought against me, but I held tight.

"I hate you," she screamed over and over.

I put my mouth next to her ear. "Well, guess what? As much as you hate me is how much I love you."

She struggled more, and afraid I'd hurt her, I let go. She spun around, fists clenched.

"Do not hit me again, Jada. If you want me to leave, I'll leave, but do not fucking hit me."

She lowered her arms and fell to her knees. "You don't love me. You can't love me. You don't even know me!" she shouted.

I knelt in front of her. "I know you better than you know yourself, sweetheart. Is that what you're afraid of? That I'll see through your bullshit?"

She raised her hand again, but I blocked her. "I told you not to fucking hit me."

Her eyes blazed in a way I hadn't seen since that first day at Butler Ranch. The first time she'd told me to leave.

"I hate you," she cried again. *"I hate you."* She covered her face with her hands and sobbed.

I managed to get to my feet, feeling the same way I would've if she'd punched me in the gut. I fell as much as sat on the sofa, remembering doing the same thing the last time she'd had that look in her eyes.

"I can't do this. I don't know how," I said, scrubbing my face with my hand.

The sound she made as she got up and came after me again, landing on me before I scrambled my way off the couch, sounded like a growl. Her nails slashed into my skin as I tried to grab her wrists to stop her.

"I knew you'd leave," she spat at me.

"Is that what you wanted?" I spat back, holding both her hands in one of mine. She'd probably have bruises on her wrists tomorrow, but I couldn't let her keep hitting me. "Are you trying to push me away? Is that it?"

She stared at me, eyes still heated.

I shook my head. "The man who fucking loves you?"

"You can't love me."

"You're wrong, because I do." I relaxed my hold when her voice softened, but I didn't let go.

"You love the person you think I am. Not me. 'The perfect Jada.' The one who's fun and laughs and never demands more than sex from you. That's who you love, not me."

I felt her muscles tense again and tightened my grip. "You're wrong," I repeated. "I told you before. I know you better than you think I do."

She shook her head. "You don't. You never even tried."

"Tried what? Talk to you? Get you to talk to me? *Fuck that shit, Jada.* We get close, then you back away and pretend like everything's fine. It isn't fine, is it? *Admit it!* Admit you can't do this any more than I can."

She fell against me, sobbing so fucking hard my own eyes filled with tears. I let go of her wrists and held her as close to me as I could. "Shh," I soothed, stroking her hair with one hand while holding her with my other arm. "God, Jada, I love you so much. I wish you could see that. I wish you could feel it."

She shook her head and whispered something I couldn't hear.

"I didn't get that, baby. What did you say?"

She raised her head and looked into my eyes. "I said I can't feel anything."

After Jada cried herself to sleep, I gathered her in my arms and carried her into the bedroom. Tonight, I stayed, rather than move to the sofa, only giving in to sleep when I couldn't hold my eyes open any longer.

When I woke the next morning, she was already up. I'd slept in my jeans, but leaned down and grabbed my shirt, pulling it over my head on my way to the kitchen. I didn't find her there, so I retraced my steps, checking the bathroom, the living room, then returned to the kitchen. I peered out the window and swore when I didn't see the golf cart parked where it had been the night before.

I pulled on a pair of boots, rushed out of the *casita*, and ran over to Tryst's place. When I knocked and no one answered, I checked the time. It was after eight. Surely, if he were here, Tryst would've heard me and come to the door.

I walked over to one of the other golf carts and saw keys in it. I started it up and drove to the barns.

"Have you seen Jada?" I shouted to Tex, who was standing in the pasture, working the same horse he was yesterday.

"Haven't. Did you check the meditation center?"

I shook my head. "On my way there now."

He nodded and waved.

As I got closer, I breathed a sigh of relief. A golf cart was parked out front. I'd found her.

I gathered myself before going inside. Last night had been rough. We'd both said things we didn't mean. Or maybe we did. Either way, we had to talk about it. We couldn't put it off any longer.

After taking several deep breaths, I got out of the cart and went inside. "Jada?" I called out when I didn't see her. The candles were lit, and there were two mats laid out on the floor. I looked over at the bathrooms, the only other thing in the open space, but both doors were open. Where the hell was she?

I pulled out my phone and called Tryst, but it went to voicemail, so I tried to reach Brix. He answered right as I was about to end the call.

"Hey, sorry," he said, catching his breath.

"Hope I didn't wake you."

"No, I've been up for a couple of hours."

"By any chance, have you seen Jada?"

"Jada? Of course I saw her."

"When?"

"Earlier this morning. She said she told you."

"Told me what?"

"She left with Press and Onyx. The plane took off over an hour ago."

"What? No. The golf cart is here. At the meditation center."

"I guess it ran out of juice. I didn't know that's where he was going when he took the truck to pick her up."

"She's really gone? She fucking left? Why didn't you call me?"

"Sorry, man, I thought you knew."

I ended the call before I said something I'd regret. I'd done enough of that. I stared at my cell in disbelief. She left. *She fucking left.*

When I raised my head, I saw a lone coyote right outside the window. It was looking straight into my eyes, just like the one I'd seen from my stairwell.

"What the fuck do you want?" I screamed at it. When it didn't flinch, I raised my arm and hurled my phone at it. Even when it went through the window, shattering the glass, the damn thing didn't move.

If it wouldn't, I damned sure would. I ran out of the building and past both golf carts. I didn't know where I was going until I reached the steps of the temple. I opened the door and went inside. I sat on the same pew Jada and I had, bent over, put my head in my hands, and cried.

It wasn't until I heard people shouting that I raised it again. I took a deep breath in and smelled smoke. That's what they were shouting. *Fire.*

I raced out the door and fell to the ground when I saw what was burning. The meditation center. Flames shot straight into the air. Within seconds, the walls caved in and it was gone.

"Oh my God," I cried, picking myself up. I knew it was too late, but I ran in that direction as fast as I could.

I was within a few yards when Tryst spun around and stalked toward me. *"What did you do?"* he shouted.

"I don't know what happened. I was looking for Jada—"

"You fucking *sonuvabitch*," he seethed, getting right in my face. "You burned down my Rosa's meditation center."

"I didn't," I shouted back at him. "There was a coyote. I threw my phone—" *The candles.* I must've knocked one over. "God, Tryst, I'm so sorry. It was an accident. I swear it."

He turned his back to me and took several steps before looking over his shoulder. "Get off my property. You are no longer welcome here."

22

Zin

I sat in Brix's makeshift kitchen after going by the *casita* and picking up my things. It was only then I'd realized none of Jada's stuff was there.

"I have to do something to make this right," I said.

"My uncle is angry, Zin. When he calms down, we'll talk to him."

"It was an accident. I swear to you."

He stood, refilled the glass of whiskey he'd poured me when I arrived, then squeezed my shoulder. "I believe you. You don't have to convince me."

I downed the liquor, and he refilled the glass. Yeah, I was getting shit-faced, but it didn't matter. Jada was gone.

"Why did she leave?" I asked for the third or fourth time.

Brix sat beside me rather than in the chair across the table, where he'd been previously. "She didn't say, and before you ask again, I don't know where she is.

My guess is she either went to her mom's house or with Onyx."

"With Onyx?"

"He said he was going back to his place in New York. Where his wife is."

If there was anywhere she knew I couldn't get to her, it was her brother's cabin in the mountains.

"Onyx has agreed to back off Los Caballeros. Between Tryst and me, we got him to relent. I also heard Doc and Merrigan refused to accept his resignation, so he's still with K19."

"I'm glad. For the rest of you."

"He was angry, Zin. He still is. However, I believe it's more at himself than at you. He came close to losing his sister the day you killed Al Zaabi. I have no doubt he wishes he could've been the one to take him out."

As Jada had, I thought to myself. "That doesn't give him the right to accuse me of raping her." I pointed to my face. "Or breaking my nose."

It wasn't Onyx I had a problem with now, though. It was Tryst. I'd never seen him act the way he did earlier. "I'm withdrawing from Los Caballeros," I said, finishing what was in my glass and pushing it toward Brix after setting it on the table.

He shook his head. "I told you Onyx has backed off."

"Tryst."

"I'll admit his behavior of late is puzzling. By that, I mean before the fire this morning."

"What's the deal with him and Jaicon? Do you know?"

He shook his head a second time.

"Hey, guys," said Addy, joining us in the kitchen. "Normally, I'd hug you first," she said to her husband. "But Zin looks like he needs it more."

I did. So bad, in fact, that I stood. She embraced me the same way my mom would if she'd been here. "Thanks," I said when she let go and took a step away.

"I wish there was something I could do to help." She walked over and sat on Brix's lap when he pushed his chair away from the table. I sat down, feeling empty— my arms, my heart, even in my soul.

"Be right back," I muttered, making it outside just before tears of self-pity fell. I walked over to the ridge and looked down at the scorched land where the med- itation center once stood and cried harder. I sat on the ground, put my elbows on my knees, and lowered my head.

How in the hell had I gotten here? A month ago, my life revolved around my law practice and Los Caballeros. Some nights, Jada stayed over, we had sex, then she either stayed another day or went home.

The "drama" in my life related to other people's, not my own. Not that any of it was easy or painless. First, Addy was arrested for murdering her stepfather. It had taken all the *caballeros* to get her cleared of the crime we knew she didn't commit. During that time, Brix had confessed the feelings he had for her. Like with me and Jada, no one had known. Except in their case, that included Addy.

Around the same time, one of Brix's brothers—Trevino—had been ambushed by a band of thugs who'd kidnapped Addy's mom. While he didn't talk much about it, Trev hadn't seemed the same since the night it happened. I shook my head. I'd known him all my life, and had I reached out to see if he needed help? Had I asked Brix about him? No, on both counts.

Then, at the Wicked Winemakers' Ball in October, the local assistant district attorney, Seraphina Reeve, had shown up and bid on Noah Ridge in the bachelor auction. After casting the winning bid, she'd begged for his help in locating her missing sister, Luisa.

Like Onyx, prior to that night, Seraphina had vowed to take down Los Caballeros. Unbeknown to us, she was being blackmailed by her boss to do so. We learned that part much later, after I'd led a witch hunt against the woman. Was that one of the sins I was now paying for? I'd been relentless in my pursuit of evidence to prove her a threat, like a junkyard dog with a bone.

The search for Luisa had brought Ridge, Press, and his brother, Beau, here to Mexico when we learned she'd been abducted by a known human trafficker and there was a chance she was being held at the port of Yavaros, less than an hour from Tryst's ranch. When the three men had assisted in a raid at the port, several other victims were rescued, but Luisa hadn't been among them.

That night, a man named Manual Varilla was taken into custody and charged with kidnapping Luisa. He was the same man Press and I had spoken of the day Jada was rescued. The one we'd vowed to hunt and kill if he was ever released from prison.

Varilla had immediately turned state's evidence, eventually confessing that Luisa was being transported out of another port in Mexico to Felixstowe, outside of London.

Most of the *caballeros* had traveled there to help with her rescue, but I hadn't. I looked up at the sky and groaned. I'd still been hell-bent on proving the woman's sister was a threat and had refused my support. I'd been such a fucking asshole.

"What's going on?" Brix asked, sitting on the ground beside me.

"Counting all the reasons karma needs to give me a kick in the ass."

"You've done more than your share of good, Zin."

I shook my head. "The bad far outweighs it."

"Is that what you think this is? Karma?"

Put that way, it sounded fucking trite. "No. Not what happened to Jada. Or Luisa."

"But what's happening to you?"

Once said out loud, I realized it wasn't that either. "I'm responsible for my own actions. I'm not saying anyone or anything else is. I do feel as though it's time I atone for my sins."

Brix raised a brow. "You've always been an asshole, my friend, but you've also always been your own harshest critic."

"I should've put Jada first. If I had, maybe she'd still be here." Maybe instead of the pain I'd witnessed last night, unleashed in anger, I could've done more to help her work through it.

"Are you sticking around?"

His question took me aback. "What do you mean?"

"Jada's gone."

I pointed in the direction of the meditation center. "I can't leave until I make things right with Tryst. If he'll let me. If he won't…God…I just don't know."

"He may not be open to it right away."

"If I take off, it'll look like I don't give a shit. I can't let him think I don't."

Brix pointed at the horizon. "Looks like a storm is heading this way. Come inside."

"Give me a minute, and I will." Instead, once I was sure he was gone, I got up and took the trail down the hillside. I was halfway to the bottom when the rain started. It sprinkled for a minute or two, then turned torrential, but I kept walking.

Once I reached the burn scar of Tryst's beloved building, I shielded my eyes against the water pelting me and walked around to where I'd seen the coyote. There, in the brush, I found my cell phone. The screen was cracked, but when I tapped it, it turned on.

There was an alert for a text message I wasn't sure I wanted to read. Whatever it was would likely make me feel worse than I already did. But wasn't that what I deserved? Shouldn't I face the ramifications of my actions head-on, regardless of how hard it was for me to do?

Jada was forced to face the ramifications of someone else's behavior. She had no option to hide from the pain. It was ever present. Even when she slept.

I walked farther, under a canopy of trees, and tapped the screen again, mindful that if I did it too hard, the whole thing might break apart, rendering it inoperable. When I saw the message was from Jada, I slid down the trunk of the tree I leaned against and read it.

I'm sorry.

That was it. No explanation. No reason for why she'd felt she had to leave. Just an apology. I raised my arm, tempted to hurl the phone into the forest, but lowered it, ashamed that I even considered repeating the action that had caused irreparable damage.

I heard a vehicle approach, but I didn't get up. If Tryst was in it, he'd probably remind me I wasn't welcome on his land.

The howling wind had shifted, and the tree I sat under no longer sheltered me from the rain pelting my skin. I folded my arms on my bent knees and lowered my head when I couldn't see through the torrent. I heard the crack of lightning followed, a split second later, by the roar of thunder. If the next bolt struck me, it wouldn't be less than I deserved.

I nearly jumped when I felt a hand on my shoulder. I looked up into the eyes of the man I wasn't sure I could actually face again. He held out his other hand and, when I took it, pulled me to my feet. Tryst grabbed my arm and led me to his truck, motioning for me to get in. I hesitated, but when he did too, I opened the door.

"I'm on my way to check on Berta."

I nodded but didn't speak.

When he reached between the seats and handed me a towel, I dried off as best I could, not that there was any hope for my soaked clothing. I thought about apologizing, but getting the seats of his vehicle wet was the least of what I needed to ask his forgiveness for.

The rain had let up by the time we pulled up to the large animal hospital, but before we got out, Tryst grabbed a jacket from the back. "Put this on," he said. I did, then followed him inside, where the vet stood waiting.

"She'll be glad to see the two of you," he said, motioning for us to follow him through a set of double doors.

"Go ahead," said Tryst when the vet led me into a room similar in size and shape to a stall. Berta lay on blankets on the floor but raised her head, then rested it on my knee when I sat beside her and folded my legs.

"Hey, B," I said, stroking her coat and wishing I had a face brush. The door opened, and Tryst handed me one as if he'd been able to read my thoughts. "Don't go," I said when he took a step backward. "She needs both of us."

Neither Tryst nor I spoke other than to Berta to soothe her. She had to be wondering why Jada wasn't with us. That she'd left her spoke volumes about how strongly she felt she had to. Only feeling as though she had no choice would've made her abandon the horse she cared so much about. I leaned down, burying my face in the horse's mane. "I'm sorry," I whispered.

I heard the shuffle of Tryst standing, followed by the sound of the door closing behind him. When Berta appeared to have fallen asleep, I gently moved her head from my leg, stood, and left the room.

"We'll keep her here another few days," I heard the vet say to Tryst as I approached. "You're welcome to visit as often as you'd like."

Tryst thanked the man, and I followed him out to the truck. We didn't speak on the return trip to the ranch, and when we reached its entrance, he kept going, pulling through Brix's gate instead.

"We'll go again tomorrow," he said when I opened the door to get out.

"Thank you, Tryst."

He nodded once, and after I closed the door, drove out in the direction from where we'd come.

When I took off the jacket Tryst had lent me and walked inside, I realized my clothes had mostly dried while we were at the vet's.

"There you are," said Addy, greeting me at the door. "Brix and I were worried sick until Tryst called to let us know you were with him."

"I'm sorry. I should've thought to do that myself."

"It's okay. Brix will be glad you're back before everyone else arrives."

I looked up at her. "Who's everyone else?"

She smiled. "The *caballeros* are on their way."

"Even the old-timers," Brix added, joining us near the door.

"Why?"

"To help you rebuild the meditation center."

My eyes opened wide. "Will Tryst allow it?"

"I think that's why your dad and the others are coming. Tryst won't be able to say no to them."

"You did this. Thank you, Brix."

He put his hand on my shoulder at the same time Addy wrapped her arms around my waist.

"Thank you," I whispered to her too.

"You did so much to help my mom and me. I don't think I've ever properly thanked you."

I'd handled the legal issues surrounding her murder charge as well as the aftermath of their dismissal. "I was just doing my job, Addy. No thanks needed."

She released her hold on me and took a step back. "Go get out of those clothes, take a hot shower, then meet me back here for lunch."

"Yes, ma'am."

She leaned up and kissed my cheek. "You probably don't remember this, but the day after I was arrested, you came to the jail to see me. Before you left, you put your hand on my arm, looked into my eyes, and promised me everything was going to be okay. You said you'd make sure of it. I felt hopeless, and your words reassured me."

She was right. I didn't remember that conversation. However, I wouldn't have said what I had unless I meant it.

Addy rested her hand on my arm. "Zin, everything is going to be okay with you too."

"Thanks." I squeezed between the two of them and hurried into the bathroom before my emotions got the better of me again.

23

Zin

The only two *caballeros* who didn't show up at the ranch were Press and his brother, Beau.

"My elder son sends his apologies and asked me to tell you he's needed in Napa presently," said Martin the day they'd arrived.

"Understood, and thank you," I'd responded. I didn't ask about Beau, nor did he offer any information about his younger son. He'd left weeks ago, after his and Press' mother passed away suddenly, saying he wasn't sure where he was headed or when he'd be back, only that he needed time. It was something those of us close to him understood. When the day came I lost either of my parents, I had no idea how I'd react. I just hoped it would be years and years before I had to find out.

All five of Brix's brothers arrived the first day, including Trevino, who I was relieved to see seemed better than the last time I'd seen him. Ridge and his brother, Bones, showed up the following day along with their father, Hewitt, Martin Barrett, and my dad. Later that afternoon, the four other men who'd been at the emergency meeting at the wine caves arrived—Baron Von Orr, George Norman, Malcolm Warwick, and Charlie Jenson.

I'd greeted each person, from the first to arrive to the last, and thanked them.

"It's what we do," more than one had responded.

We spent the first two days clearing the debris from the fire. On the third, George—the sole architect in the group and a man familiar with the Vastu principles so important to Tryst, laid out the plans he'd drawn up to rebuild the center.

"We're going to raise the foundation," he explained when we gathered around him. "The previous structure was built on a concrete pad. By reinforcing it the way we intend, it will allow us to add heat beneath the floor as well as provide better comfort in other ways."

"What are these?" I asked, pointing to two rooms on the opposite side from where the restrooms had been before and would be again.

"Sacred rooms," Tryst said from behind me. I hadn't seen or heard him approach. "You and I will be the only two working on their construction."

Before I could ask anything further, not that I would have, he returned to his truck. I turned around to study George's plans when I heard him call my name.

"It's time to visit Berta," he said, motioning for me to join him. I looked over at Brix.

"Go with him," he said.

I bit my tongue several times on the way, wanting to ask about the sacred rooms he'd mentioned, then talked myself out of it, knowing if Tryst wanted to share that or anything else, he would, just like he had—or hadn't, since he rarely spoke at all—every time I rode with him to the large animal hospital.

"We'll be moving Berta to a rehab facility later today," the vet said when we were leaving after spending over an hour with the horse.

"To the ranch?" I asked.

Tryst shook his head. "She will need more care than we are able to give her at this time."

I wanted to argue, to tell him I'd care for her, but I couldn't. My place, for now, was at the construction site.

On the return trip to the ranch, my mind drifted to Jada like it did so many times throughout the day and especially at night. Brix was the only person I'd asked about her. He'd assured me she was safe and not alone, but otherwise, offered no further information. I respected that, knowing if he could tell me more, he would.

With the number of people on the building site, including those who worked for Tryst both at the barns and on other parts of the ranch, we made tremendous progress each day. By the end of the first week, the foundation was laid, the framing was complete, and HVAC, plumbing, and electrical had been installed. Next would come the insulation, then the drywall.

"Come with me," said George when we were wrapping up that day's work. I followed him away from the building site and in the direction of the temple. "Take these inside," he said, handing me a rolled set of plans before turning around and walking in the opposite direction.

When I opened the heavy wooden door, Tryst was facing the altar, his back to me. I hadn't been in the temple since the fire. With each step I took, my legs grew heavier with the weight of my actions that day.

I cleared my throat to make sure he'd heard me. He glanced over his shoulder and motioned for me to join him. I set the roll of plans on the pew and stood next to him.

"I owe you an apology," he began.

"Tryst, please—"

He held up his hand. "Allow me to finish."

I nodded.

"I have been struggling for some time now with my own feelings of betrayal. I made a vow to Rosa to love and honor her every day for the rest of my life and forever, into eternity. I have not kept my promise or my commitment to her, and for that, I am filled with regret. More, I am ashamed."

I couldn't help but wonder if he was alluding to whatever was going on between him and Jaicon. I hadn't known Rosa, but I would be surprised if she'd meant for Tryst to spend the rest of his life alone.

"What you experienced was anger at myself directed at you. It was unfair—wrong—of me."

I waited for him to continue and, when he didn't, asked if I could speak.

"By all means," he said, looking into my eyes. My voice was choked with emotion by that alone. The relief I felt was profound.

"While the fire was an accident, my actions, my anger, caused it, and I take full responsibility. I know

I can never make it up to you, Tryst. Please just know how sorry I am."

He nodded, turned to the altar, and closed his eyes. Was he praying for forgiveness for himself? For me?

I bowed my head and closed my eyes, too, praying for both of us, whether he was or not.

I couldn't remember ever saying a prayer before Jada brought me to this temple. Even then, I don't think I had, at least not purposefully. I had the day of the fire, though.

When I opened my eyes, Tryst was studying me. He put his hand on my arm. "I forgive you, Vaile. Now you must forgive yourself."

Like so many other times over the last few days and weeks, I was on the verge of tears. "Thank you," I whispered.

"That is the hardest part—forgiving ourselves."

"It is." I let out the breath I hadn't realized I was holding.

"I believe there is a way to make it easier for both of us." He walked over to the pew, motioning for me to join him. He removed the band and unfurled the papers George had asked me to bring inside. "These are the sacred rooms I asked to be included in the new center.

One will be named for Rosa. The other is up to you. We will work together on them. Just the two of us, and only when the others have finished for the day."

"Okay."

"Spend the next few hours, days if you need to, meditating on what you would include in the room in order to honor the person whose name you choose."

Of course I would honor Jada, but I appreciated Tryst allowing me to make the decision for myself. Or at least, I believed he was.

He rerolled the plans, put the band around them, and handed them to me.

"The hardest day of my life was when I had to say goodbye to my Rosa. Part of me wanted to go with her, and part of me wanted to beg her not to go. She had to. She'd been hanging on for me, and that wasn't fair. I loved her enough to finally realize I had to let her go."

I didn't need to ask Tryst if he was comparing his wife and him to Jada and me. I knew he was. I also knew he thought it was time I let Jada go. He stood, but I remained seated. "I need a few minutes," I said when he walked toward the door.

"Take all the time you need, son."

24

Jada

I'd done little other than cry since the day Press brought me to stay at his family's estate in Napa. He and Luisa had given me space, not asked me to explain or even talk. All they'd said was they would do whatever they could for me. The problem was, I had no idea what that was.

While at the ranch in Mexico, I'd put on a brave face and woke up each morning pretending to be the same person I was before my abduction. Except I wasn't, and while I'd said those words to Zin, it wasn't until I arrived here that I truly felt them. Truly understood what they meant. And that was, I didn't know who I was.

I thought about the last night Zin and I were together, or at least had tried to. There was so little I remembered. All I knew, when I woke in the middle of the night and saw him asleep beside me, was that I'd hurt him. Said things to him that were almost worse than the way I'd attacked him. I'd hit him, and not just once.

I'd gone after him over and over again. I told him I hated him. Not once. Many times.

I rolled to my side on the bed I'd hardly left and sobbed. The pain I felt was excruciating. Unbearably so. And none of it had anything to do with the now-almost-healed wounds on my chest and torso. It was deep, deep inside me and felt like the glass I knew was shattered had broken apart, its sharp shards cutting into me when I so much as took a breath.

I closed my eyes, again picturing Zin soundly sleeping beside me. I remembered praying so hard, when I eased from the bed and gathered my belongings, that he wouldn't wake up. If he had, he would've tried to stop me from leaving, and I had to. I couldn't trust myself around him ever again. What I'd done was so horrifying, so unspeakable, and yet, I feared losing control and it happening again.

The man had done nothing to deserve the anger and violence I'd forced upon him. He'd saved my life. My fucking life. The one I no longer recognized. The one I wished he hadn't. If Al Zaabi had killed me that day, there'd be no pain for me to feel now. And Zin? While he would've been devastated, at least then he could remember the woman I used to be, not the vile, evil, filthy person I'd become.

I rolled from the bed and went into the bathroom, turning on the shower I'd gotten out of less than an hour ago after nearly scrubbing my flesh raw. I would again, as soon as the water was hot enough. No matter how hard I tried to clean the despicableness from my flesh, no more than an hour later, I could feel it spreading again, covering me like a thousand insects.

I leaned over the toilet, retching the meager contents of my stomach, mostly bile now since I hadn't kept food down in days. I wiped my mouth and opened the shower door when the steam clouded it from the bottom to the top. I slid down the tile wall and reached for the bodywash I barely had the strength to pick up. Maybe if I turned the temperature of the water up, it would wash away the filth I no longer had the ability to scrub.

"Jada! Open the door!" I heard someone shout. Had I fallen asleep? I must have. My skin was bright red from the scalding water that now felt cold. How long had I been in here?

"Jada, I'm coming in!" a different voice shouted. Press. Before, it had been Luisa. I tried to cover myself, but I didn't have the strength to even raise my arms.

The bathroom door burst open. Press rushed in first, but Luisa was right behind him. He reached in and turned off the water while she grabbed a towel, got in, and covered me with it.

Press gathered me in his arms and picked me off the shower floor. "Call an ambulance."

"No!" I screamed, using what little energy I had to fight my way out of his arms. "No," I said again rather than screamed. I didn't have the strength.

He set me on the bed, and Luisa covered me with the sheet and blanket. I closed my eyes, praying the sleep that eluded me would finally come. Praying I'd exhausted myself to the point I'd pass out like I must have in the shower.

"This can't go on," I heard him whisper. "She needs medical attention. It's been a week, Luisa. She isn't eating; she isn't even getting fluids. She *needs* medical care."

"I'm calling Bones," Luisa whispered back.

"Good idea," he responded, now from the other side of the room. "I'm sure he'll suggest we take her to the nearest hospital."

"No, Press," she argued, still in a hushed voice. "She's staying here. You saw her. Going to a hospital terrified her."

"But it's what she needs," he implored.

"What if it were me in that bed? Would you have forced me?"

I opened my eyes, watching as he shook his head.

"Whatever you would have done for me is what we're going to do for Jada." She lowered the phone. "There was no answer."

"I'll ring Doc," he said, leaving the room and closing the door behind him.

Luisa's eyes met mine. She rushed over to the bed and sat beside me. "You aren't going to the hospital, Jada. I promise. I won't allow it. But you do need help I can't give you."

My eyes filled with tears, and I shook my head, wishing she could understand I didn't want help. I wanted the pain, the nightmares, the horror not just of what Al Zaabi had done to me, but of what I'd done to

Zin to go away. If only I could slip into unconsciousness and never feel any of it again.

I closed my eyes when I heard footsteps, then the door reopened. Luisa's weight left my side, and I listened to her footfalls walk in the other direction.

"Bones is in Mexico. Doc is on his way, but he won't arrive for at least two hours. He fears she's severely dehydrated and asked if we could try to get her to drink something."

"We can try," Luisa whispered. "But I don't want to leave her."

"No, you shouldn't. I'll bring something up."

I heard the scrape of a chair being dragged closer to the bed, then my friend's stuttered breath. I looked into her tear-filled eyes, wishing I could stop her pain, but I couldn't. No more than she could stop mine.

"Sweetheart, I need you to try to take a couple of sips." I opened my eyes to see she held a glass of water. "Just one or two to hold you over until Doc gets here."

I nodded, rose up as much as I could, and did as she asked when she brought the glass to my lips. I closed my eyes again after she set it on the bedside table.

I must've fallen asleep, but woke when I heard Press' voice. "I think we should call Zin."

"No!" I shouted, trying at first to get out of bed, but only getting as far as sitting up. "You can't call him. Please don't call him," I begged.

"He won't," said Luisa, rushing over and taking my hand. "Doc is coming, and that's all. Okay?"

I nodded and let my eyes drift back closed.

When I woke again, Doc was there. I knew him more as Kade, though.

"How are you doin'?" he said, tapping my arm with his fingertips. "You need some fluids, so I'm trying to get an IV started."

"You don't have to…"

Kade squeezed my hand. "I do, sweetheart, and you may not believe so right now, but the day will come when you think back to the conversation we're having and you're going to be glad I did."

I'd been so focused on his eyes, his words, that I hadn't felt the needle even go into my arm until he said, "There we go." He taped the IV site and attached the fluid line. "You're gonna feel a lot better real soon, Jada."

"How do you know I'll be glad?" I said, barely above a whisper.

Kade took my other hand and brought my index finger to his face, using it to trace the outline of the scar that ran from the side of his mouth across his cheek and almost to his ear. Then he raised his shirt and pointed at the marks dotting his chest and abdomen. "I've been where you are. And someday, you'll be where I am now." He pulled out his phone, swiped the screen, and held it out for me to see. "That's Merrigan, my wife, and Laird and Rielle, our son and daughter. I also have another daughter, Quinn. She's the mother of my first grandchild, a little girl named Elisabette." He held up another photo.

I brushed at the tear running down my cheek. "What if I never…" I couldn't say the rest.

"It wasn't your time, Jada. That's why Zin was there that day. Your life was spared—saved—because you have more living to do. You have purpose, sweetheart. The day you wake up and realize what that purpose is, is the day you'll look back to the conversation we're having right now and be so very happy we did."

While I appreciated what Kade was trying to say and do, just because his life had turned out so perfectly, it didn't mean mine would. Same with Luisa. She'd found Press, who adored her just the way she was.

It was different for me. Zin had never known the real me. I'd never given him the chance. Maybe if I had, he could help me find my way back. At least part of the way. But how could he? How could I? If there was one turning point to me proving to myself I wasn't the person I believed I was, it was my last night with him. I'd said and done things I never thought myself capable of. Until I was sure I'd never do it again, it wasn't just Zin I couldn't be with; it was anyone. That's the part Kade didn't understand and never would. Neither would Luisa. No one ever would.

25

Zin

It was exhausting, helping rebuild the meditation center during the day, then staying behind after everyone else had left to work on Jada's sacred room. Not that I was getting much work done.

I'd asked Tryst for guidance on what to include, and he'd responded that the walls were empty to allow me to do whatever I felt would honor Jada best. I knew better than to ask what he was doing in Rosa's room since he locked the door when he wasn't there and, once he went inside to work, kept it closed.

The only guidance he had given me was to tell me I could do anything I wanted. I could paint the walls, build things, bring in furniture, artwork—in the same way I would if I were decorating a room in my house.

I'd spent the first two nights sitting on the bare floor, staring at the blank walls. I thought about Jada, both before her abduction and after, about the ways she was the same and those she was different.

She was the same *person* I first met at the radio station when she was sixteen. When we met again, she was older, different certainly, becoming a woman rather than a teenager. The first time we'd kissed, she was different too. She'd aged and matured in the years between.

I thought, too, about the things she'd said to me the last time I saw her—after I told her I loved her.

"You love the person you think I am. Not me. 'The perfect Jada.' The one who's fun and laughs and never demands more than sex from you. That's who you love, not me."

My response had been that she was wrong. I *did* know her, and I *did* love her—at least I thought so.

I pulled out a notepad, planning to write down every detail about the woman I could think of. First, Jada loved to laugh. She loved sex too. Those were two things a person couldn't fake.

She cared about her family, even when they made her crazy, and had always had a soft spot for the under-dog, people in pain, those less fortunate than she was. Her life's mission was championing them.

She was smart. Far more intelligent than she gave herself credit for. And she loved the outdoors. Even when the weather was chilly, she'd pull me out the French doors that led to the lawn. We'd spread a blanket on the ground, and that was where we'd stare up at the night sky, watch for shooting stars, talk, and make love.

Jada and I hadn't just fucked. We'd loved on each other, our bodies communicating the emotions neither of us was brave enough to speak.

I thought about the room where she slept in her mother's house. I'd only set foot in it one time, when Esmeralda was visiting her sister and Jada and I knew she wouldn't be back for a few hours.

It wasn't *her* room, though. She'd shared the small space with her sisters, growing up. When they moved out, her mother had told her she could redecorate, but Jada had said it wasn't important to her.

I looked down at the notepad where I hadn't written a single word. I didn't need to. In my heart, in my soul, in my mind, I knew her. I also knew exactly how to honor her.

I got to my feet, went out my door, and knocked on Tryst's.

"Yes?" Tryst said from behind it.

"I have a question."

"One moment." He came out, trying to keep me from seeing inside.

I smiled at his secrecy, almost like a parent wrapping Christmas or birthday gifts for their young kids.

"What would you like to know?"

I motioned him into the still-empty room. "Am I limited to within the four walls?"

He cocked his head. "What do you have in mind?"

"I want to add a door here." I pointed to the exterior wall. "I want to extend the space outside."

Tryst smiled and nodded. "Speak with George and explain what you'd like to do. He will assist."

This time when I returned to the room, I closed the door and called my mother.

"Hello, sweetheart," she said, answering on the first ring. "How are you?"

"I'm sure Dad has kept you abreast of how I truly am. However, I'll say this; I'm getting better."

After she told me how happy that made her, I told her the reason for my call. "I need your help with something." I gave her the basic rundown, the dimensions she had to work with, and ended the call after she said she'd get started on it right away.

After jotting down a few more measurements along with a list for George, I walked out of Jada's room, shut the door, and grabbed a blanket from the back of the nearly completed main meditation room. I took it outside, spread it on the ground, and lay down.

You love the person you think I am. Not me. She was wrong. I knew her, and until the last hour, I hadn't realized how well.

When I heard rustling in the brush, I propped myself up on my elbows. "I was wondering when I'd see you again," I said to the coyote who had crept within a few yards of me. "Have you come to give me my lesson?" The animal didn't get any closer. Instead, it lay on the dirt and appeared to sleep.

After watching it for a minute, I dropped my elbows and stared up at the sky. Soon, my eyes drifted closed like the coyote's had.

I pictured Jada. It was a breezy summer day, and she wore a yellow sundress. Her long brown hair hung loose, the way I liked it best. She was twirling on the grass, her long legs were tanned from the sun, and she was barefoot. Her smile spread across her face, and she laughed. It sounded like the most beautiful piece of music ever written. She waved, and while I wanted to approach her, my feet wouldn't move. It was as though they were stuck in cement.

She took a few steps in the opposite direction, then turned and blew me a kiss. Two steps more, and she faded into the horizon, almost like a ghost.

I woke with a start and looked over to where the coyote lay. It was on its feet now and, like Jada had, turned and walked away. After a few steps, it looked over its shoulder, just briefly, then continued walking into the darkness of the night until I couldn't see it anymore.

I heard the words Tryst spoke in the temple as if he were sitting beside me, repeating them. "The hardest day of my life was when I had to say goodbye to my Rosa. I loved her enough to finally realize she was waiting for me to let her go."

I knew then I wouldn't see the coyote again. Its message had gotten through. I'd finally heard it. As hard as it would be for me to let Jada go, I had to. Until I did, she couldn't move on with her life. And neither could I.

It took another couple of days for George and the crew to install everything I'd asked for, both inside and out. The only thing left was what my mother was working on. It would take several days to complete, and Brix had agreed to take care of it for me once it arrived.

With little left to do, I went to visit Berta at the equine rehab facility. I was stunned when I arrived and saw her standing in the pasture.

"She's doing really well," said Tex, approaching me.

"What are you doing here?"

"Didn't Tryst tell you? She's been adopted. I'm here with the trailer to deliver her to her new home."

My heart clenched. "He didn't mention it."

"It's a good day for ol' Berta. Not that she's old. She's got a whole life ahead of her, being cared for by someone who loves her." Tex whistled, and Berta slowly made her way to the fence.

"Can you give me a minute to say goodbye?"

He got a funny look on his face, then nodded. "Sure, I've got a couple of minutes. Not much longer than that, though. I gotta get on the road. Long drive ahead of me."

I didn't ask where Berta was going. I didn't want to know. Like with Jada, even with the coyote, our time together had come to an end. All that was left was to say goodbye.

Three days later, I packed my stuff, said so long to Brix, Addy, and Tryst, then boarded the plane that would take the other *caballeros* and me to California.

I was sure I'd visit Tryst's ranch again one day. I hoped Jada would too. I'd love for her to see the space I'd created to honor her, even if I couldn't be there when she did.

26

Jada

Lynne arrived the day after Doc put the IV line in and had remained since. "I'm a pushy New York broad," she'd said more than once in the days that followed. "I'm not gonna quit naggin' you until I can get some nourishment in you that doesn't come through a tube."

Yesterday, she'd finally removed the IV, which meant I'd be on my own since there was no need for me to be under her care any longer. However, she'd threatened to put it right back in if she got wind I wasn't taking in enough nutrients.

While I would've preferred to stay in bed most days, she'd put a stop to that too. Or more than two showers a day—one in the morning and one at night.

The wounds on my body had healed. I had scars, but not as many or as bad as I'd anticipated. Lynne had given me a salve to put on twice a day that she said would help them fade.

Before she left, I asked about the ranch and, after I had, regretted it.

She said there had been a horrible accident and the meditation center had burned to the ground. She didn't know the details of how it had happened but thought it might have been caused by lightning.

I couldn't imagine Tryst's devastation. He'd built it for Rosa, and there were reminders of her throughout the space. I found myself relieved I hadn't witnessed it.

Like with Luisa, my first thoughts were of how I wouldn't have been able to bear the pain of it, rather than how much Tryst needed my support and comfort. I stood and walked over to the window that looked out over the vineyards. The sun was bright, and I could see my reflection in the glass almost as clearly as if I was looking in a mirror. Had I always been this selfish? Always been more concerned about myself than those around me who I supposedly cared about?

I picked up my phone, intending to call Tryst and tell him how sorry I was to hear about the fire, when there was a knock at the door.

Luisa came inside when I called out for her to. "I need you to come downstairs with me."

"I really don't feel up to it." I held up my phone. "I was about to call Tryst."

"There's something I need to show you. After I do, you'll want to call him even more."

I hesitated, looking between her and my cell.

"*Please*, Jada."

I took her arm when she offered it, and we walked down the staircase.

"Well, what is it?" I asked when we reached the bottom and she stopped.

"Hang on." She walked over to the coat closet and handed me a jacket. "Put this on."

"We're going outside? Luisa, I really don't feel—"

She took both my hands in hers. It was something I'd seen her and Press do when one was trying to impress something on the other. "I know you're going to want to see this. Just be patient for a few more minutes."

I'd just put on the jacket when Press opened the front door.

"Are we ready?" Luisa asked him.

The way he looked at her when he smiled and said they were, nearly broke my heart. Press loved Luisa so much. It hurt to think I'd never have that in my life. I shook my head and squared my shoulders. I couldn't continue to wallow in self-pity. Eventually, I would let go of the dreams I'd had before Al Zaabi stole them from me and move on with my life. I had no choice. The only other option was for me to give up my will to live. Over the last few days, it had become clear to me that no one here would allow me to do that.

"Come on." Luisa tugged me to the door. "Now, close your eyes."

"Seriously?"

"Please!"

I did as she asked and let her lead me outside.

"Okay, open!"

"What in the world?" I gasped. Only a few yards in front of me stood Tex. Berta was beside him. I raced over and threw my body against hers. "How?" I asked, looking between Tex and Luisa.

"I'd like to take credit, but it was actually Tryst and Press who did it," she said.

"How is she?" I asked Tex.

"We took our time getting up here, so she's hanging in. A little better than me, I think."

"There's a stall ready for her in the barn," said Press, joining us. "I'll give you a few minutes, then we can walk her over there if you'd like."

I threw my arms around him. "Thank you for doing this. I can't begin to tell you what it means to me."

He leaned back. "And I can't tell you how nice it is to see your smile."

Press led Tex inside to get him something to drink while Luisa and I stayed with B.

"I can't believe she's here." She nickered when I rubbed my face against hers. "And she's *standing*!"

"She's also yours, Jada."

"What do you mean?"

"Exactly what I said. She belongs to you. She'll stay here as long as you do, and when you leave, Brix said you can board her at Los Cab. Not that I'm in any hurry for you to go. You can both stay forever as far as I'm concerned."

I hugged her. "You're such a good friend to me, Luisa. I wish I was a better friend back."

Her eyes filled with tears, and she shook her head.

"I'm sorry. Did I say the wrong thing?"

"I could say the exact same thing to you. You've always been so good to me. When no one else was, you were. There isn't anyone who's a better friend to me."

She was wrong, but I wouldn't argue with her now. I was too happy to see Berta.

When Tex came out saying Press was going to get him settled in one of the guesthouses for the night, I bit my tongue to stop myself from asking about Zin. Did he know Tex had brought B here? Had he suggested it? Probably not. If he had, either Luisa or Press would've said so.

"I've been workin' her a good bit over the last couple of weeks. Her leg seems really strong."

"I heard about the fire."

Tex took off his hat and wiped his forehead with the back of his arm. "Hell of a thing. When I left, they were just about finished rebuilding, though."

My eyes opened wide. "Already?"

"Yeah, a bunch of guys flew down to help. One was an architect. Anyway, I've never seen a building go up as fast as that one did. And no expense was spared either. Zin made sure of it."

"Zin? Was he still there?"

"Still is, I think. There's no way he'd leave before construction was finished."

"Why not?"

Tex studied me. "I thought you knew. The fire was his fault."

"What do you mean?"

"I don't know the details. No one would talk about it. Tryst hardly talked at all for the first few days. Now that it's almost finished, he seems better. He sure perked up when the vet told him Berta was well enough to travel. First time I'd seen him smile in days."

My heart ached for Tryst and for Zin. If the fire really was his fault, I knew he'd never forgive himself.

Zin came off as arrogant and self-centered, but he wasn't. And while I'd given him shit about the kind of lawyer he was, over the years, I'd learned how much pro bono work he did.

If any of his friends or their families needed legal help, he was always there for them. When Brix's now-wife, Addy, was charged with murder, Zin had made arrangements for her to stay in the holding cell in the small town where she lived rather than being transferred to the county jail in San Luis Obispo. That night, he'd requested the judge arraign her first thing in the morning, and while few knew this, he'd given his personal assurance she would not skip bail.

I was ashamed I'd never truly thanked him for saving my life. From what Press and Luisa told me, he'd crawled into the drop ceiling of the underground radio station and, as soon as he'd had a clean shot, killed Al

Zaabi. It had to have taken great courage for him to do that—to shoot another human being. I'd been so busy pushing him away, worrying about myself, that I hadn't realized how that one act would affect the rest of his life.

In the little we talked about it, the only thing I'd said was that it had to have been traumatic. I hadn't asked how he felt, whether he'd had nightmares, or whether he regretted his actions that day.

Like me, no one seemed to appreciate it either. When he came face-to-face with Jaicon, she'd been cool and distant to him. And Montano, my God, he could've killed him, the way he went after him in that stall, throwing him up against its wall. I doubted very much my brother had apologized to him either.

"You're quiet," said Luisa, who stood on the other side of B, stroking her like I was.

"I'm thinking about Zin," I admitted.

"I'm sorry I didn't tell you about the fire. At the time, you were—"

"You did the right thing by not bringing it up then. I was spiraling downward, Luisa."

"I know," she whispered.

I saw the flash of pain in her eyes. I knew she felt guilty about my abduction, felt as though it was her fault. We hadn't talked about it other than when she brought it up the first day at Butler Ranch, and we needed to. There were so many things we needed to talk about, including what a shitty friend I'd been after she was rescued. Like Zin with the fire, it was something I'd never forgive myself for.

When Tex asked if I was ready to take Berta to the barn, I told him I'd show him the way. Luisa said there was something she needed to talk to Press about and went inside.

I wanted to ask him more about Zin, but I didn't. Instead, we walked in silence.

"I'll be back in the morning," I told her after checking with Tex to make sure she'd be okay on her own overnight.

"She's been living the normal life of a horse," he assured me.

I took a shorter path to the main house after Tex also assured me he could find his way to the guesthouse.

When I walked in through the kitchen door rather than going around the front, I heard Press and Luisa talking.

"It's your decision, my darling," he said.

"I don't feel right having a wedding right now. I always dreamed Jada and my sister would stand up with me if I ever found a man who loved me enough to ask me to marry him."

There was a pause in the conversation, and I had no doubt they were kissing.

"Valentine's Day seems too soon."

"I want you to be happy, Luisa. That's all that matters to me."

Rather than pretend I hadn't heard their conversation, I walked through the kitchen and in the direction of the voices.

When Press saw me, he excused himself.

I squared my shoulders, walked over to Luisa, and put a smile on my face. "You're getting married? I'm so happy for you."

Her forehead furrowed. "I'm sorry I didn't tell you. I seem to be saying that a lot lately."

I did my best to exude happiness. "And on Valentine's Day? How wonderful."

"It was one idea. I think we're going to wait until the weather is warmer, though. We've talked about having it at Seahorse."

Seahorse was Press' oceanfront estate near the seaside village of Cambria on the Central Coast of California. This time of year, it would be chilly outside. "You could have it inside," I suggested.

"We wanted the ceremony to be on the beach."

"Luisa, I know the temperature isn't your reason for delaying."

She led me into the solarium, one of my favorite rooms in the house. It had once been a porch, but Press' father had it enclosed so it would be used all year. The exterior wall was constructed in a semicircle made almost entirely of windows that looked out over the vineyards. I understood why she and Press would want to have the ceremony on the beach; however, this would be a beautiful spot too.

Before she could speak first, I did. "We have so much we need to talk about."

"We do. I wasn't sure if this was the right time."

"I think if we don't, we'll keep putting it off."

She looked away when her eyes filled with tears. "I'm just so sorry."

"I am too."

Luisa turned back toward me. "You don't have anything to apologize for."

"You're wrong. I have a great deal I need to get off my chest, so to speak. I guess being able to joke about it means I've made some progress."

"Talking with a counselor helped me so much, Jada. I'm not sure if that's something you want to do."

A week ago, my knee-jerk reaction would have been to say I didn't. However, I felt more receptive to it now. "I'll need to find someone."

"I like the woman I've been talking to. Most of the time, anyway." Luisa laughed. "Sometimes she pushes me to talk about things I know I need to but would rather not."

"That would be me with everything." I thought about a conversation I'd had with Zin. I'd said I'd rather bury my head in the sand and forget everything that happened. He was Mr. Fix-it, and neither of us could slide dealing with our shit into our comfort zone.

"There's one thing she said to me that I find myself coming back to over and over—" I reached out and covered her hand with mine when she choked up. God, I wished I had done that more often, then listened to what she needed to say rather than telling her we didn't have to talk about whatever it was if it was too upsetting.

"She said I'd never go back to my idea of normal again. Being kidnapped and dumped in a shipping container with other victims, traveling across an ocean, and not having any idea of the horrors that would face me wherever I was going, changed me. I'd never look at myself or life the same way again."

I nodded but couldn't speak when my eyes filled with tears.

"But—"

"I'm so glad there's a 'but.'"

"I'm broken, Jada. You are too, but that doesn't mean we can't be put back together. We may not look or feel the same, but we will be whole again."

"I wish I could believe that's possible."

She squeezed my fingers. "It is, but it takes work. I won't lie and say it isn't hard. Sometimes, it does feel impossible. The important thing is I keep going. Keep trying to put the pieces of myself back together."

"I wouldn't know where to start."

She looked beyond me, and when I turned my head, I saw Press standing in the doorway.

"My apologies for the interruption."

"It's okay. I was about to tell Jada something you said to me I'll never forget." She motioned for him to join us, then turned back to me after he sat down beside her. "When I told Press what I just told you, that I felt as though my life was in pieces…" She turned to him.

"I told you I wanted you to look at yourself, accept yourself, the same way I did."

She nodded. *"Beautifully broken.* That's what we are, Jada. Right now. It doesn't matter where we think we are on the journey. We aren't working toward anything more than accepting the beauty in who we already are."

Press stood and excused himself.

"I'm not a counselor or an expert, but I believe the next step, for both of us, is forgiveness of each other and of ourselves."

"I'm sorry I wasn't a better friend to you, Luisa."

Her mouth hung open. "When was this? Because I don't remember a single instance when you didn't put me before yourself."

"When you got back from England, and then when you had to leave Seraphina and Ridge's wedding early."

She cocked her head. "You were with me both times. Jada, you gave up your life for me."

"But…I never asked."

"Asked what?"

"About what happened to you. What you went through. I never even asked if you wanted to talk about it."

This time, her forehead scrunched. "I thought you just knew I didn't. God, everyone wanted me to talk about it. With you, I could just be. You and Press were the only two people who allowed me to get out of my head for a while."

She sounded sincere, but she could just want to let me off the hook. "I feel like I should've done more."

"You've always done more for me than anyone else. *Anyone.* That includes my own family. When everyone at school bullied me, said I should've died in the car crash my father caused rather than the four people who did, you stood up for me. You stood *next* to me. You never left me alone. From what I remember, you got permission to switch your schedule so it was the same as mine." She squeezed my hands. "And how did I repay your kindness? You were kidnapped and tortured because of me. I'm so sorry, Jada. I don't know how you'll ever forgive me."

I shook my head. "Not because of you. Because of a fucking lunatic psycho. You had no control over what he did. You didn't even know. And as far as forgiving you. You're right. I won't, because there's nothing to forgive. You weren't any more responsible for what happened to me than you were for your dad driving drunk."

Luisa smiled through her tears. "You've always been so easy on me."

"That's because you're never easy on yourself."

"Right back at ya, girlfriend."

27

Zin

Tomahawk and I began pruning the vines the day after I returned from Mexico. We weren't finished, but we were close. He'd offered to have his crew take over for me after the first week, but I refused. "I'll get faster. Bear with me," I'd joked, and I had.

Besides the vineyard workers and Tommy, I didn't see too many people. Brix and Addy were still in Mexico, and Press was in Napa with Luisa. Ridge and Seraphina had invited me over for dinner twice, but when they did again this week, I thanked them but declined. I wasn't in the mood to see anyone, particularly not a newly married, wildly in-love couple.

I missed Jada every minute of every day. It had been six weeks since I last saw her. Six weeks since the night that almost destroyed us both. I'd asked Brix about her three times, but the last two times, his response had been the same. "She's with people who love her." More than I did?

Besides missing her, there was one thing that nagged at me. A few days after I got home, Tommy asked if I'd thought any more about why the coyote had visited me. While he was talking about the one here at the vineyards, I told him the whole story of what had happened in Mexico—the last night with Jada, the fire, all of it, including what I'd determined the lesson was.

I expected him to agree or at least comment, but he hadn't. In fact, all he'd done was say, "Hmm," in a way that made me think he didn't agree. When I asked him what he thought, he said it was between the coyote and me.

On the walk back to the house today, I wondered, like I had several other times, about the lone coyote I saw here. Was it still around? Had it been accepted into the pack?

I pulled my cell out of my pocket when it vibrated, expecting it to be my mom. While I'd told her it wasn't necessary to call me as often as she did, I had to admit hearing from someone helped me not get too caught up in my head.

"Hey, Press," I said when I saw his name appear on the screen.

"Zin, my apologies for not getting in touch sooner."

"Is everything okay? How's Luisa?"

"Fine, fine. She's fine."

I rolled my eyes but kept my mouth shut. His tone of voice alone gave me cause for concern.

"Listen, there's a reason I haven't been in contact, and I fear when you hear it, you'll be quite angry. However—"

"Spit it out, Press. Whatever the hell it is."

"Jada is here with us. She has been since we left Mexico."

He was right. I was angry that my best friend hadn't put his loyalty to me above Luisa's loyalty to Jada. However, as he'd begun to say, if he had asked me what to do, I would've told him Jada and whatever she needed to do or wherever she needed to be was all I cared about.

"Zin?"

"I'm here. Why are you telling me this now?"

"She asked I contact you."

There were times when the way Press dragged things out made me crazy. *"About what?"*

"Jada would like to see you if you're willing."

Willing? Of course I was willing. "How is she?"

"Much better than when she arrived. We were quite concerned for a while. Nonetheless, she's making progress. Luisa is as well. I believe they've both managed to find closure with certain things in their lives. Jada has been seeing a therapist recommended by the one Luisa meets with, and I believe that has been a tremendous help."

"Why does she want to see me?"

"I'm aware of the events of the night before she left. Not in detail, but enough to know things were left unsettled between the two of you. I believe that's her reason for asking me to make contact on her behalf."

Fuck! There were so many things about this conversation that tempted me to hurl my phone across the lawn in the same way I had that day at the meditation center. Instead, I gripped it tighter. "When?"

"As soon as is convenient for you."

Convenient? Jesus. "Sure. I'll let you know when I can make arrangements."

I was about to end the call when I heard Press say my name.

"Yeah?"

"I want you to know how sorry I am."

It was a dick move, but I hit end without responding.

I didn't call him back the next day or the one after that. On the third day, it occurred to me that if I hesitated too long, Jada might ask Press to rescind the invitation.

"I'll fly up tonight, stay with my folks, and if it's *convenient*, come by tomorrow morning. How's ten?" I said when Press answered my call.

"Looking forward to seeing you," he said.

I couldn't say the same. I dreaded going to Napa and seeing Jada. It was why I'd put it off. Until she actually said she didn't want me in her life anymore or ever again, there was a small part of me that held out hope. Based on the few things Press had said about how she was able to find closure, I was sure that's what this visit was about. If it were for any other reason, Jada would've contacted me herself. More, I would've heard something from her before now. The last time I had was from a text saying she was sorry. That's it. Sorry. It still felt like a knife in my heart whenever I thought about it. And I did far more than I should allow myself to.

I was about to phone my parents when I received a call from my mother.

"I'm flying up tonight if that's okay."

She nearly squealed. "Of course it's okay. I've been pestering your father about coming to visit you. Is there a particular reason, or do you just miss us?"

I smiled. "I miss you, Mom. I miss Dad too. However, Jada is at the Barretts'. She's asked to see me."

My mom was quiet long enough that I wondered if she'd known she was there. Was I the only one who hadn't?

"Mom?"

"Sorry, sweetheart. I just feel for that poor girl. What happened to her is horrible."

"I'll see you tonight. I love you, and tell Dad I love him too."

Because I was an only child, or maybe it was just how my parents were, saying I love you had always been the way our calls ended. I'd once thought if I had kids myself, I'd make the same rule, not that I considered that a possibility any longer.

I walked over and sat on the porch steps. By this time tomorrow, things would be over between Jada and me—once and for all. I dreaded it more than I had anything else in my life, no matter how much I'd accepted it had to happen.

I went inside, tempted to get drunk in a way I hadn't since I got home. I didn't, though. Tomorrow, I had to have my wits about me enough to mask the heartbreak I knew I'd feel. I spent the rest of the time before my flight figuring out what I'd say, how to make it easier for both of us.

My first few attempts sounded too much like the closing arguments in a trial. Finally, I came up with something I could get through. It was short and concise, with as little emotion as possible, given I'd be saying goodbye forever to the woman I loved.

I was on my way to my car to catch my flight when I saw something in the woods. A fucking coyote.

"Look, I got the other message, okay? I get it. I'm not going to beg her not to end things."

The damn thing just stared at me, even after I'd gotten in the car and drove past it on my way to the airfield.

28

Jada

"Zin will be here at ten tomorrow morning," Press said, coming into the solarium, where Luisa and I were sitting.

At least, he'd finally heard something from him. When two days went by without a word, I figured he saw no reason to ever talk to me again. It shouldn't have come as a surprise, given how I'd treated him that night, the things I'd said and done. And how I'd left the next morning without contacting him since except to say I was sorry.

I'd asked Press not to tell anyone I was here, and after I did, there were a thousand times I wished I hadn't. If he'd known where I was, would Zin have shown up here like he had in Mexico?

The only exception had been my family. My mom and sisters came to visit, and my brother said they would, but this was a busy time in the vineyards, so I understood why they hadn't. When I explained to them that no one could know I was here, I let them believe it was for my safety, even though I hadn't said it specifically.

"How are you doing?" Luisa asked, looking down at my wringing hands.

"I'm okay."

"Just speak from your heart. That's all you can do."

"Wanna go for a ride?"

Luckily for me, Luisa almost always said she wanted to when I asked. However, I felt bad about the amount of time I took her away from Press. Neither made me feel as though I was overstaying my welcome, but I was beginning to think I was. My options for where to go if I left were limited.

I couldn't go home. I mean, I could. I would be welcome there, but being that close to where Zin lived worried me. I also wasn't sure how I'd feel about driving down the road where I'd been abducted. Considering it was the only way to get to my mom's house, I would've had to.

Onyx told me more than once I'd be welcome to stay with Blanca and him, but I wouldn't have felt comfortable. I also wouldn't have known what to do about B. I didn't want to be away from her for any length of time, and there was nowhere near their place where I could board her. Not that I had the money to.

Finances were the reason I couldn't find a place of my own, either. If I couldn't afford to board my horse, how would I pay for an apartment for myself? As it was, Press paid for everything Berta needed. I'd thought about offering to reimburse him, but how? I doubted he'd let me work for my room and B's board.

By this time tomorrow, maybe I'd have a better idea—or any idea—of what the next steps in my life would be.

I slept fitfully at best, finally getting out of bed at seven to go to the barn. B would be happy to see me and wouldn't mind if I talked both her ears off.

"Today's the day, girl. Zin is coming. I hope you get to see him too. I know he'll be happy to see how well you're doing."

When she nickered and bumped me with her face, I giggled. How long had it been since I did? I couldn't remember.

By ten, I was waiting in the solarium, first sitting, then pacing, then sitting again. Luisa stayed with me until we heard Zin arrive.

"Remember, speak from your heart."

I nodded. "I will."

Zin came around the corner, and my heart nearly stopped. He'd only gotten handsomer since I last saw him. He looked like he'd spent time in the sun, and his muscles seemed to stretch the fabric of his dress shirt more than I remembered. The only thing missing was his smile.

"Jada," he said, looking down the length of me. "That dress…"

I looked down at the yellow sundress I was wearing. Maybe it was too much. On the other hand, he was wearing a button-down shirt. I wanted to ask if he liked it, but based on the look on his face, he didn't.

"Do you want to sit down?"

"For a minute. I can't stay long."

I felt my stomach sink.

"You look good, Jada."

"Thanks. You do too." I cleared my throat. "So, um—"

"Let me go first."

"Okay. Sure." I sat on the sofa, hoping Zin would too, but he remained standing.

He squared his shoulders as if he were in a court-room, then cleared his throat like I had. "Jada—"

He may as well have started with, "Ladies and gentlemen of the jury."

"I meant what I said when I told you I loved you. I still do, love you. I always will, and if you ever need anything, anything at all, I'd be more than happy to give it to you. What I'm trying to say is I'd really like to be your friend, Jada. I understand we aren't right for each other, but that doesn't change how I feel. How I'll always feel."

"That you want to be my friend?"

"Yes. If you do, I mean."

He'd gone from sounding like an attorney to a frat boy, so anxious to end the conversation that he was falling over his words.

"Was there anything else?" I asked.

His eyes scrunched. "Um, I don't think so."

"Okay. Well, thank you for coming all this way." I stood to see him out.

"Was there anything you wanted to say?" he asked.

I shook my head. "No, I think you about covered it."

He leaned forward and kissed my cheek. "Bye, Jada."

"Bye, Zin."

I walked him to the door and went directly upstairs. I'd wanted to run, but didn't. Once there, I grabbed my cell.

"Jada, how nice to hear from you," said Tryst.

"Hi, um, I have a favor to ask."

"Anything."

I blinked away tears, hoping I could hold it together just a little while longer. "Can I come back to the ranch?"

"Of course. You know you are welcome here anytime."

"It's more than that, Tryst. I want to come there to live. Berta too."

"I see."

"If it's too much—"

"It isn't too much. I will make the arrangements. I'll call you back in a few minutes and let you know when Tex will arrive. Will that be okay with you?"

I nodded, even though he couldn't see me. "Yes," I managed to eke out.

"Good. I'll call you shortly, little one."

"Tryst? Thank you."

"You're welcome."

I hung up, grabbed my bag out of the closet, and packed the few things I'd brought with me. I didn't know when I'd be leaving, but regardless, I wanted to be ready.

When I heard her knock, I shouted for Luisa to come in.

"What happened? He wasn't even here ten minutes."

"He said he'd always be my friend. That was the gist of it. And now, I'm moving to Mexico."

"Oh, Jada, I'm so sorry."

I didn't want to cry, but I couldn't hold it in any longer.

29

Zin

Why did she have to be wearing that fucking yellow sundress? Getting the words I'd practiced saying a hundred times or more out was the hardest thing I ever did. Keeping my eyes from wandering down to that dress had given me a headache. Headache, heartache. Hell, my whole body ached, down to the tips of my toes.

Once I was out of the Barrett Estate gate, I pulled the car over. My hands were shaking, and I felt nauseated, so I rested my head against the steering wheel.

"I think you about covered it," she'd said after I confessed I'd love her forever, would do anything for her, and my feelings for her would never change. *You about covered it.* Jesus.

I raised my head when I heard a horse whinny. I looked across the road, and there by the fence, stood Berta. Did I dare get out and see her? How could I not? It might be the last time I ever saw her.

I climbed out of the car and ran across the road.

"Hey, sweet girl," I said when she put her head down for me to rub between her eyes. "So this is where Tex brought you. Very nice." I reached up and put my arm around her neck. "Listen, B, I need a favor. I want you to take really good care of our Jada. Will you do that for me?"

Berta nickered and nudged me with her face.

"Yeah, you want more love, but I gotta go." I bit my tongue to stop myself from dissolving into tears, ran back across the road, got in the car, and returned to my parents' house.

"How'd it go?" my mom asked when I came in the front door. "You weren't gone very long."

"She didn't have much to say."

My mom rushed over and hugged me. "I'm so sorry, sweetheart. Did you get a chance to ask her about the mural?"

I shook my head. "No. I'm sorry."

"It's okay. I was just anxious to hear what she thought of it."

"I don't think she's seen it yet."

My mom's mouth twisted. "If she had, I'm sure she would've had a lot more to say."

I hugged her tight. "It's okay, Mama Bear. Your little boy's gonna survive."

"I know. I just don't like to see you hurt."

"Part of life, right?"

"Not if I had anything to say about it."

I stayed with my parents overnight only because my mom would've worried if I hadn't. The following morning, I told them I had to get back to work, though.

My dad offered to take me to the airfield, and on our way, we passed a dually hauling a horse trailer. I could've sworn the guy driving was Tex.

"Everything okay?" my dad asked when I turned to look over my shoulder.

"Yeah, just seeing things."

"Happens more and more the older you get, son."

30

Jada

It was a twenty-two-hour drive from Napa to Tryst's ranch in Mexico. Fortunately, Tex was able to fly up and use a trailer one of Press' neighbors was selling to transport Berta. We made two stops along the way. First, just south of Santa Barbara, then in Tucson. Tex found places where we could stay and board B.

By the end of the third day, when we pulled into Tryst's *El Lugar de Curación,* we were equally exhausted and elated.

"Welcome home, little one," Tryst shouted, running over to me when we pulled up to the barn.

"You're good for my soul, Tryst."

"As you are for mine. Perhaps you'll even call me 'uncle' again." He winked.

"I don't know how to thank you for letting me come back and bring Berta with me. I want you to know I'll do whatever you need to earn my keep and B's. I can work in the barn, work with horses, clean the main house and the *casitas*, cook, mend fences—"

"Slow down, Jada." Tryst laughed.

"I don't want you to think I expect to live here for free."

He put his arm around my shoulders. "After Berta is settled, let's go into town and have dinner." He turned to Tex. "Please join us."

Tex said he'd be happy to get my horse settled and, after that, even happier to go home, take a hot shower, and sleep until dawn.

"I should never have left," I murmured on the drive from the ranch to the town of Alamos.

"You did what you needed to do at the time."

"I was so sorry to hear about the meditation center."

Rather than look sad, Tryst smiled. "Wait until you see it. It's even better than it was before the fire."

"But…Rosa…"

"There are many ways I honor my Rosa on the ranch, and while some of the physical things may be gone now, there are many more in their place."

"I'm glad you feel that way, Tryst."

He pulled up to a restaurant that could only be described as a hole in the wall.

"Okay?" he asked, motioning to it.

"Better than okay. Looks like my kind of place." And Zin's. He loved spots like this one. Not that we'd ventured out to many, especially close to home. We'd gone on one road trip in the four years we hung out together. We spent the first night in Tehachapi, and the second in Lone Pine. Every time we'd stopped to eat, it was at a location that looked a lot like the one we were about to walk into.

On the third day of our trip, we'd hiked Mt. Whitney. It was one of the best adventures of my life.

"Whatever you're thinking about is a good memory, little one."

"It is. I just wish I'd made more of them when I had the chance."

"I know the feeling well."

"I was thinking about something on the drive down here. After we'd crossed over the border," I said once we'd ordered dinner and were enjoying a *cerveza*.

"Go on."

"You know I graduated with a law degree but haven't taken the bar."

He nodded.

"The reason I didn't take it right away was because I hadn't decided what kind of law I wanted to practice."

"Have you now?"

"I read about trafficking victims and how many of them start out as immigrants but run out of means to continue their journey, especially while traveling through Mexico."

"It was the case with many of the victims rescued from the same ship Luisa was on. It made reunification especially difficult."

"I'm thinking about immigration law," I blurted.

"A noble pursuit, and an area where I believe you will excel."

"There's no bar exam in Mexico."

Tryst smiled. "I believe you'll find yourself quite busy in the days and weeks to come."

When we returned to the ranch after dinner, Tryst asked if I'd prefer to stay in the main house or a *casita*.

"The house, if you don't mind."

He raised a brow. "What I mind is how often you say 'if you don't mind.'"

Tryst was already gone when I got up the next morning. After making coffee and getting something to eat, I took the golf cart sitting outside the door to the barns, where I checked on Berta.

While I knew she was comfortable and happy in Press' barn in Napa, she seemed more relaxed here, with other horses she knew.

Rather than take the golf cart, I walked to the meditation center. If I hadn't known about the fire, I probably wouldn't have spotted the signs of it on the ground and in the brush near the building. However, I would have noticed the center had been rebuilt.

I felt the same sense of peace the minute I walked in the door, but it felt more soothing. Instead of carpet, beautiful hardwood floors had been installed. When I lay the mat out, I noticed they were warm to the touch.

Where before there were two bathrooms on one side of the main room, there were now two more doors opposite them. I went to check to see what they were, but both were locked.

I meditated for thirty minutes, did a light workout, then walked to the temple. I glanced up at the ridge where I'd seen the man I didn't realize was Zin. There was no one standing there today.

The temple, like the meditation center, was soothing, but I carried an uneasiness inside me I'd hoped would go away the longer I was here. I knew it was about Zin; however, things between us were settled. We'd both gotten closure, and now it was time to move on with the rest of our lives.

Having something useful to do would certainly make doing so easier. I hoped.

31

Jada

Eight Months Later

In order to become licensed to practice law in Mexico, I had to do two things. First, I was required to volunteer at a law practice for no fewer than four hundred hours. There was a firm in the town of Alamos that desperately needed assistance and was more than happy to allow me to work in their offices for as many hours a week as I'd like.

The second requirement was performing three hundred hours of social service. Most of that I'd been able to do on the ranch, working with Tryst's equine rehabilitation program. While I'd initially thought I'd prefer training horses, after the first week, I found I much preferred helping people who came to the ranch to heal. People like me.

Horses were highly sensitive to those around them and were quick to react to sudden changes in their environment. The program Tryst and Rosa had developed was initially for men and women with a terminal illness. Like Rosa.

By demand, it had expanded to serve those dealing with depression and anxiety, particularly teenagers. The benefits of spending time with a horse were immeasurable. By being around the animals, teens' self-esteem improved and they were able to build confidence. Since horses were so sensitive to mood and subtle changes in people close to them, those in the program learned the importance of nonverbal communication and behavior modulation.

Most importantly was trust. Many of the teens who came to the ranch had suffered abuse, trauma, or abandonment. Like Berta had with me, the horses helped heal those emotional wounds.

Between my hours spent at the law practice and then with the equine rehab program, I had little time for anything else. I managed to get to the meditation center every so often and to the temple once a week. Otherwise, I studied for the exams I needed to take to get my legal license after I fulfilled the other requirements, and I slept. I rarely even saw Tryst unless he was at the barns or returned to the main residence before I went to bed.

Yesterday, though, I'd completed the hours at the law firm. I'd finished the social service work a few weeks ago, but I loved doing it so much that I'd continued going to the barns daily.

"Good morning," said Tryst. "What a pleasant surprise to find you still here on a weekday."

"I'm done at the law firm, so I slept a little later today."

Tryst poured himself a cup of the coffee I'd made and sat at the dining table. "I'm proud of you, little one. You've worked so hard."

I thanked him, but I didn't feel like I had. Maybe because I enjoyed what I was doing so much, it hadn't felt like work.

"We have a special visitor arriving any minute— your cousin Alex."

She was my only female cousin, and I'd admired her all my life. Alex took no shit from anyone, but she also had the best sense of humor of anyone I'd ever met.

"What's the occasion?" I asked.

Tryst shook his head. "She has been pestering me to be in the bachelor auction at the Wicked Winemakers' Ball. Thus far, I have been able to convince her I cannot do it. I fear her visit is to persuade me I can."

"That's next week, isn't it? It doesn't seem possible." The ball was held in October after the grape harvest and crush ended. It raised upwards of a million dollars each year to support the children's hospital in Paso Robles. I'd never gone as a guest, but had worked as a volunteer after Alex took over as chair of the event five years ago.

"Time flies when you're as driven as you've been."

Thankfully, I'd been too busy to think much about the time of year, although it lingered in the back of my mind. Crush, or harvest season, was the most hectic and chaotic time of the year in the wine industry.

Picking operations took place twenty-four hours a day at the bigger estates. At the same time, the harvested grapes were delivered to the wineries where they were "crushed" to be made into wine.

It began in August and sometimes stretched into November, but on the Central Coast, it typically wrapped up by mid-October. By the time the last of the grapes were picked, everyone in the industry was dead tired but ready for a party.

Zin and I had shared our first kiss at such an event ahead," he said, shutting it behind me once, held that year at Butler Ranch. Three years later, we spent our first night in each other's arms. Every year after, we'd attend, acting as if we were acquaintances rather than lovers. At the end of the night, we'd meet back at his place and spend the next two or three days in bed. God, I missed him.

While thinking about him didn't hurt as much as it had when I first returned to the ranch, I still ached, particularly after I dreamed he and I were back together.

It was what I'd wanted the day he came to see me at Press' place. I'd planned to confess I loved him and beg him to forgive me for what I'd done that night at the *casita*, and to give us another chance.

Instead, in a matter of minutes, he told me he'd always loved me even though we weren't right for each other, but hoped we could be friends.

As much as I shouldn't, I couldn't help but wonder who he might be kissing at the crush party this year.

Tryst stood when Brix's car pulled up. "Here she is now."

Alex swept inside like the force of nature she was, embracing Tryst when he met her at the door, then rushing over to me. "Can I hug you?" she asked.

"You better." I smiled and opened my arms.

"Damn, it's good to see you, girlfriend. I've missed you so much. Oh, by the way, Brix said to apologize, but he was meeting a contractor at the house this morning and had to rush off. He said we'd see him and Addy later."

"I'd forgotten how much the two of you look like sisters," Tryst commented.

"I'll take that as a compliment, although I'm not sure Alex would," I teased.

She put her hands on my shoulders. "Jada, you are so beautiful. You always have been."

Beautiful? More like beautifully broken, I thought to myself.

Tryst walked over and put his arm around my shoulders. "Our Jada has trouble accepting praise."

"Thank you," I said to her, my cheeks turning pink at Tryst's admonishment for not doing so.

"The thing about you, Jada, is you're just as lovely on the inside as out. Of all our cousins, you've always been the kindest, the most helpful, and the most giving."

I shook my head. "You must be thinking of one of my sisters."

"Right. The sisters who haven't helped once with the winemakers' ball, yet you put in countless hours before, during, and after."

"She has been helping with the equine program," said Tryst, squeezing me. "The visitors love her."

"I'm not surprised. You've always been selfless."

My eyes scrunched, and I twisted away from Tryst.

"What's up?" Alex asked.

"I'm not, and I haven't been. I mean, I'm learning to be, but I'm not selfless."

She shook her head. "It's always the ones who are who don't see it." She nudged Tryst. "How can we prove it to her?"

He smiled at me with such warmth in his eyes. He wasn't my father's brother, but he so often reminded me of him. "Perhaps it's a good day to visit the meditation center."

"I would *love* that!" Alex exclaimed.

Tryst turned to me. "Jada?"

"I'd love it too. If I had the time, I'd spend every morning there. I've missed it so much."

"Can we go now?" Enthusiasm gushed out of my cousin for *everything*. It was one of the ways I wished I was more like her.

The three of us piled into the golf cart and went straight there. "Later, we'll visit the riding center," said Tryst when we drove past the turnoff.

Alex clapped. "I'd love that too!"

A sense of peace washed over me as soon as we pulled up to the building. It had been at least two weeks since I'd been here. Maybe longer.

"It looks amazing!" said Alex when Tryst led us inside. "What are those?" She pointed to the north side of the space and at the two doors I'd wondered about. The last time I was here, they were plain. Now, they had elaborately carved signs on them.

"These are sacred rooms," Tryst explained when we followed him closer to them. He motioned to the door on the left. "This is named for Durga, the goddess of protection and strength."

I studied the words on the wooden sign. *"Om Shree Durgayai Namah,"* it read. It was Durga's mantra.

Tryst motioned to the other door. "And this is named for Mahadevi, the Mother Goddess." Her mantra was carved into the wood like Durga's had been. "Would you like to see inside?"

"Of course." Alex was more subdued than she had been. Probably, like me, she innately knew Mahadevi was how Tryst saw Rosa.

"Jada, I will let Alex into this room first while you visit Durga's."

I thanked him and waited as he unlocked the door and motioned for her to go inside. Then he unlocked the second one. "Go ahead," he said, shutting it behind me once I'd crossed the threshold.

The room was much larger than I'd expected, bigger than my bedroom at my mom's house. There was a French door leading out to a small garden. From where I stood, I could see flowering vines in all my favorite colors—blue veracruzana, orange trumpet, and red, magenta, and orange bougainvillea.

I slowly turned in the space big enough for two people to meditate on the open wooden floor or in the overstuffed chairs. One wall had a Vastu altar, or Mandala, where several candles surrounded the idol Durga. I faced the wall behind the door and gasped.

There was a floor-to-ceiling mural of the same deity painted on the wall. Except, rather than look like other paintings I'd seen of Durga, the woman in the mural looked just like me. And rather than seated on a lion or tiger, as she typically was, she was astride a horse—one who looked like Berta.

I sat in one of the chairs positioned to face it and studied the image. In her ten hands, Durga held the ten things normally associated with the goddess—a conch shell, a discus, a lotus flower, a sword, a bow and arrow, a trident, a mace, a thunderbolt, a snake, and a flame, all elaborately painted in bright colors. Behind her stood two children, something I'd never seen in a depiction of her.

The door eased open, and Tryst came inside. He sat in the other chair.

"It's so beautiful, but I don't understand," I said, turning to him.

He held out an envelope. "Perhaps this will enlighten you."

I stared at it but didn't take it from him. "I'm afraid."

"There is no need to fear love, little one."

He stood, set the unsealed envelope in my lap, and left the room. I took out the folded paper and began reading.

My Jada, my love,

I cling to the hope that the first time you see

this room honoring you, I'll be with you. It's the fear I won't that leads me to write this.

Simply, I want you to know how much I love you. How much I have always loved you. I will continue to do so for the rest of my life and into eternity.

I'm sorry I wasn't brave enough to acknowledge my feelings for you sooner than I did. More sorry I didn't confess them to you until it was almost too late.

The mural you're looking at was painted by my mother. However, the vision it depicts is from my dreams.

Jada, you are the embodiment of strength and protection. Both of those traits saved Berta. She knows it as well as I do, and it's why I chose her to carry you on your journey.

I am in awe of you and have been since the day I first saw you as a woman rather than a child. My life, my world, came alive that day.

The love you give so freely was something I

once took for granted. No longer, though. I understand its rarity.

Above, I said the image you're viewing came from my dreams. You, Berta, and the two children I asked my mother to include in the mural were with me. When I woke, I realized I'd just witnessed what heaven must be like.

If I'm not with you today, know it's where I wanted to be more than to take another breath.

I love you, Jada. I want to spend my life with you if you'll only have me.

All my love, affection, and honor,

Zin

I remained in the room, reading Zin's letter so many times I knew it by heart. "Come in," I said when I heard a knock at the door. Tryst sat in the other chair like he had before and took my hand in his.

"I wish you weren't crying," he said.

"I wish I could understand."

"The letter didn't explain?"

"If anything, it confused me more," I admitted.

"Would you like to talk about it?"

I nodded. "If you wouldn't mind."

He cocked his head and smiled. "What did I tell you about saying that?"

"You wished I wouldn't. I'm sorry. I won't do it again."

He squeezed my fingers. "Tell me what's on your mind, little one."

I told him every word of what Zin had said to me that day in Napa and what I'd planned to say before he arrived.

"Why did you allow him to leave without telling him how you felt?"

"Because he said he understood we weren't right for each other."

"And you did nothing to convince him he was wrong."

"Tryst, he rejected me!"

"He told you he loved you and he always would. I may be wrong, but I would guess the letter said the same thing."

"He said he wants to spend his life with me." I put the letter back in the envelope. "What if I'm too late?"

"You aren't."

"How do you know?"

He stood and pulled me up with him. "Let's talk to Alex."

When we came out of the room, she was standing near the windows with her back to us. When she turned around, I saw she'd been crying.

"Maybe this isn't a good time," I whispered.

"For what?" she asked.

"How is Zin?" Tryst asked her. "Have you seen him recently?"

"Ugh. That man. Yeah, I've seen him. I'm one of the few who have. I practically had to get down on my knees and beg him to be in the auction. He finally said yes, and honestly, I think it was because he just didn't care enough to argue with me any longer."

"Why? I mean, why are you one of the few who's seen him?" I asked.

"I have no idea what happened in the last six months, maybe longer than that, but Zin seems to have given up on everything. He closed his law practice. He was working in the vineyard for a while, but Tomahawk had to call in help from us and some of the other win-ery owners when Zin was so inconsistent. He'd show up one day, but not the next."

"Alex, do you know that prior to this year, Jada and Zin were seeing each other?"

I glared at Tryst, then looked at Alex.

"You have?" she gasped.

Tryst nudged me. "Tell her how long."

"Four years," I muttered.

"How did I not know about this?"

"No one knew."

Alex put her hand on her hip. "Yeah, but I'm not no one."

"It sounds to me like Zin is heartbroken."

"Uncle Tryst, you are worse than my mother. Jada's too."

"What?" he said, holding up both hands.

Alex shook her head. "What about you? Are you heartbroken too?"

"Yes," I admitted.

"The two of you remind me of Maddox and me. Both so stubborn. Anyway, who's going to make the first move? Are you, or are you going to hide out in Mexico like Zin's hiding out in Paso Robles?"

"I'm not sure what to do."

Alex tapped her cheek. "God, it's so simple. Perfect, really. Come on, we've got work to do."

I let her pull me out of the meditation center, only realizing once we were on our way to Tryst's house that I hadn't seen the other room.

"I know I said I was going to stay over, but we need to get home," Alex said once we were partway there. "That includes you."

"Me?" Tryst asked.

"Yep. You owe me one, and I'm cashing in. You will be in the auction next weekend."

He raised a brow. "I owe you one? Remind me, niece, what for?"

"For getting Jada and Zin back together again."

32

Zin

I thought about telling Brix I was unable to attend the emergency meeting he'd called tonight at the wine caves. It would be the first time Los Caballeros would be together, officially, since the night we'd believed Onyx Yáñez had enough on us to take us down.

However, if I didn't show, I'd be the only one who wouldn't. Press told me his brother had returned and even he was going to be there. Maybe I'd ask him where he'd been for the last several months and disappear there myself.

When I entered the meeting room, I walked over to my designated seat at the large round wooden table and stood behind the chair. I would remain standing until Brix, our senior-most member, arrived to call the meeting to order. Before he did, no one would speak or even make eye contact.

Admittedly, when I first became a member of Los Caballeros, I'd thought it was hokey, but the older I got, the more I appreciated the customs and traditions.

Since I didn't have to make small talk tonight or respond civilly when someone asked how I was, I especially appreciated it.

I looked down at the table, part of me hoping that whatever we were meeting about meant I wouldn't have to attend the Wicked Winemakers' Ball this weekend or be in the bachelor auction. I still couldn't believe Alex had talked me into it. I'd finally agreed just to get her to leave me the hell alone.

As she'd said, it was one date, and not an official one, at that. I'd been in the auction before; I knew the drill. It was up to me to come up with an itinerary those attending the ball felt compelled to bid on. Mine usually involved a private dinner at the winery either preceded or followed by an outdoor concert or balloon ride or something else equally trite.

I had no idea it would be this year because Alex had offered to put it together for me as long as I agreed to show up.

Brix entered the room last, then made eye contact with each person standing at the table. Once he had, we took our seats.

"I appreciate all of you coming on such short notice. I'm sure you'll all join me in welcoming Beau back. We've missed you, brother."

Beau nodded and, like Brix, met the eyes of everyone in the room.

"We have received information from our friends at K19 Security Solutions. One of their teams, Allied Intelligence, has been investigating the trafficking ring responsible for the abduction of both Luisa Reeve and Jada Yáñez."

My gut clenched at the mention of Jada's name. Had the traffickers been responsible for what had happened to her, or had it been the work of one man? Since I'd killed him, we'd never know.

"According to the brief Press is handing out, Manual Varilla and Hamad Al Zaabi were both recruiters for a specific group of traffickers." I opened the report, but closed it when Brix stopped talking. He cleared his throat, took a deep breath, then looked at Press, who had remained standing. His hands gripped the chair in front of him.

"My apologies," he began, clearing his throat the same way Brix had.

"I can continue," Brix offered.

Press shook his head. "One moment." He let go of the chair and stood up straight. "In an interrogation that took place earlier this week, Manual Varilla confessed that he and Hamad Al Zaabi were recruiters for traffickers of high-end sex slaves sold on a dark web auction site." His eyes met mine. "According to Varilla, Luisa was—"

I pushed my chair back and rested my forearms on the edge of the table as a wave of nausea radiated through my body. I didn't need Press to say more. I doubted anyone in the room did.

"What is the purpose of the emergency meeting?" asked Kick, Brix's youngest brother.

Brix opened the file in front of him. "According to K19's sources, there are known associates of both Varilla and Al Zaabi active in the area. With eight colleges and universities on the Central Coast, along with an increased migrant population due to the seasonal work at the vineyards and wineries, there is an abundance of recruitment options this time of year."

"God Almighty," muttered Ridge, seated between Brix and me.

"I don't mean to be disrespectful, but again, why the emergency meeting?"

Brix nodded at his brother. "K19 will have a presence at the auction this weekend."

"Why?"

"They have their eyes on a man they believe will be in attendance. They've asked for our support."

"What about the auction?" Kick asked.

"If you're suggesting it be canceled, I'll let you be the one to propose it to our sister," Brix responded.

"Will Alex be aware of any of this?" Ridge asked. It was a question I had as well.

"She will not."

"Is that our job, then? To run interference between them?" Kick asked.

"If you mean K19, then yes. At least in part," said Brix.

"Luisa and I will not be in attendance this year," said Press, pulling out his chair to take a seat. "In fact, we'll be returning to Napa at the conclusion of this meeting."

I didn't blame him. I hoped that was where Jada was too. To be sure, though, I'd ask.

Until now, I hadn't. I didn't want to put Press in the middle of her and me, given the last time I saw her, at his house, we'd ended things. Or I did. Only because I knew she would, and I couldn't sit through the agony of her "letting me down easy."

"Jaicon Heart, who many of us have met previously, will be our point person this weekend. She's requested we meet her an hour before the event starts. She'll give a more in-depth briefing then."

When Brix adjourned the meeting, I made a beeline over to Press.

"Do you have a minute?"

He raised a brow. "Do you have to ask?"

I led him out of the meeting room and into another of the cave's barrel areas. "I'm sorry to bring this up, and I don't want to put you in an awkward position. I'm just confirming that Jada is still staying with you and Luisa."

Press shook his head, and his eyes scrunched. "She left the day after you saw her."

"To go where?"

"Mexico. She's been living at the ranch with Tryst."

"Good. I mean, it's good she's not here."

Press put his hand on my shoulder. "I agree, mate, and while I never said this, I'm sorry things didn't work out between the two of you."

"Me too."

33

Jada

"You're sure this will work?" I asked Alex for the tenth time.

"I did it last year for Brix and Addy, so yes, I'm sure."

The plan was that Alex would guarantee I'd be the winning bidder when Zin stepped on the stage of the bachelor auction. When I asked about the money the charity would lose from this, she told me not to worry about it. Given I couldn't afford to bid as much as one hundred dollars and I knew the "dates" usually brought in thousands of dollars, I had two choices. I could hang on to my pride and refuse to let Alex help me, or I could go along with her plan and maybe—just maybe—work things out with Zin.

Keeping myself busy waiting for the bachelor auction to start was easy. I'd never been a guest at this event. While my main job was to remain out of sight so Zin didn't see me, there were still things I could do to help Samantha Marquez, Alex's lead assistant.

Thankfully, she was aware I needed to remain behind the scenes.

"You could keep an eye on the electronic sheets for the silent-auction items and start adding table positions for the highest bidder," she suggested.

"Perfect." I went into the office and started organizing the sheets. When there was a knock at the door, I froze. No one was supposed to know I was here. What if someone had alerted Zin and he was looking for me? I rolled my eyes. That was ridiculous. Even if someone had informed him of my presence, why would he come looking for me? He'd ended things between us months ago.

Rather than call out for whoever it was to come in, I remained silent, hoping they'd go away. When the door handle turned, I panicked. Should I hide under the desk? There wasn't anywhere else I could.

"Can I help you?" I asked when a man I didn't recognize stuck his head in the door.

"I'm looking for the organizer. I didn't receive a bid paddle."

"Oh, um, well, it's a bachelor auction. That may be why."

He raised a brow, and I realized my *faux pas*. Maybe the man did want to bid on a bachelor.

"Samantha Marquez can help you. If you ask any of the other volunteers, they can point her out to you."

Rather than thank me or leave, the man came inside. When he shut the door behind him, I heard the lock click.

34

Zin

"Where is she?" Alex asked Sam, who had been making notes of the paddle numbers of bidders. I was a few feet in front of them, but I wasn't the only person who'd heard her. Alex had forgotten to turn her mic off.

"Sorry, everyone. I'm looking for Petra. Has anyone seen her? She's handling the phone bids."

I glanced over my shoulder in time to see Sam mouth, "Petra?"

"Just go along with it," Alex whispered to her.

Being on this stage felt awkward every year I'd done it, but none more so than right now. Something was up, and I was front and center while everything appeared to come to a standstill. "You either explain what's going on right now, or I walk off this stage," I said, making my way over to the two of them. "And you better tell me the truth, Alex. You're a horrible liar."

"Jada's here. She's supposed to be bidding on you. I'm sure everything's fine. She probably got waylaid or is still in the office and hasn't realized the bidding began."

Jada was here? Time slowed to a screeching halt as I surveyed the silent crowd staring at us. I jerked away from Alex, whose hand was on my arm, and jumped off the stage. At the same time, I saw every one of the *caballeros* in the audience stand.

"The office," I said through the comms Jaicon had outfitted us with an hour before the event began. The din of the attendees questioning what was happening was growing increasingly louder as I rushed through the maze of tables.

When I reached the hallway that led to the office, I saw Jaicon standing right outside the closed door, holding a gun. "Support needed in the back hallway," she said through the comms.

"Jada?" I heard her call out. "The bidding has started. Are you coming out?" She looked down at the door handle and shook her head. Did that mean it was locked?

"Sorry. Be right there," Jada responded.

I drew my gun like she had and nodded.

"You cover Jada," she whispered.

I nodded once and moved aside when one of the guys on Jaicon's team ran up.

"Count of three," Jaicon whispered, motioning for him to bust through the door. While I'd heard her words clearly, the next she spoke were muffled by the sound of my blood racing through my body.

When the door broke from the hinges, the first thing I heard was Jada's scream. The second was Jaicon yelling, *"Freeze!"* at the man I only got a glimpse of before focusing on Jada.

She stood right in front of me, eyes wide. Everything else faded away, sounds, sights, everything. I grabbed her around the waist, picked her up, and ran as fast and far away from the office as I could. She clung to me, her arms wrapped around my neck so tightly, I struggled to get a deep breath.

I came to the end of the hall, pushed through the heavy exit door, and got out into the parking lot. I had no idea where I was going except that I wanted to get her to a place where she'd be safe.

"What's going on?" she asked.

I didn't know where to begin. Truthfully, I had no idea, except Jada wasn't where Alex thought she should have been. The office door had been locked, and three people with guns, myself included, rushed in once one of them broke the door down. Rather than answer, I turned my head and kissed her cheek.

We were within a few feet of my car when I heard Brix shouting my name. I glanced over my shoulder and saw him running toward us.

I set Jada on her feet, unlocked and opened the door, then helped her inside. After closing it, I walked around to the driver's side.

"What happened?" Brix asked.

"I'm not sure. I just want to get Jada out of here."

"Right. Go. I'll see what I can find out."

Jada stared out the window the entirety of the two-mile drive to my house. Once there, she waited for me to open her door, then took my hand and followed when I led her inside.

"Can I get you anything?" I asked.

"Got any bourbon?" Her eyes looked everywhere but at me.

I pulled out the bottle and two glasses, poured some for both of us, and handed one to her.

"Cheers," she said before downing the shot I'd poured her. When she pushed it over to me, I studied her, not knowing what to make of her behavior.

"So, um—"

Jada motioned for me to pour, so I did, but I set my own glass on the counter.

"Are you okay?" I asked.

She raised her glass to her lips. "I will be after this. Maybe one more."

"Do you want to talk about what happened?"

She cocked her head, and her eyes met mine for the first time since we came inside. "What happened?"

"At the ball? In the office?"

I watched her pull out a stool and sit at the counter. "I'm not sure I know." When she turned her head and looked out the window, I got between her and it.

"Will you look at me?"

Her eyes met mine for the second time. "Can you give me a minute?"

I put one hand on her shoulder and cupped her cheek with the other. "Dammit, Jada…" I struggled to keep my voice even. "For the second time, I rescued you from danger. You wanna know why? It isn't because I have some fucking hero complex. I did it because I love you. I love you with every single breath I take. It doesn't matter if you're in Napa or Mexico or anywhere else in the world; I still love you. I think about you all the time. *All the fucking time*. And I don't really give a shit anymore if you think we don't belong together, because we do, and I'm prepared to prove it to you if you'd just stop pushing me away."

Her eyes remained riveted to mine. One side of her mouth upturned like the beginning of a smile.

I leaned in closer. "Do you understand what I'm saying?"

"There's a lot I don't understand, but that? Yes."

"And?"

Jada removed my hand from her cheek, leaned forward, and kissed me.

I kissed her back like a starving man, devouring her lips and her mouth. I reached around her and put my hands under her bottom. When I lifted her, Jada wrapped her legs around my waist.

I carried her out of my kitchen and up the stairwell. Our mouths stayed pressed together—molding, coaxing, insistent, and so fucking hot, I wanted to set her on the top stair, strip our clothes off, and bury my cock deep inside her. But there was a reason I'd carried her out of the kitchen and was about to take her into my bedroom. Once in my bed—our bed—I wanted to keep her there for as long as she'd let me. Preferably forever.

"Jada—" I groaned when, after I'd set her on the bed, she began unfastening the buttons on her blouse. I wanted to move her hands out of my way and do it myself, like I always had. There'd rarely been a time when I hadn't removed every stitch of Jada's clothing before we had sex. I loved doing it, loved when her eyes focused on mine as I slowly stripped away every barrier to her body. By the time I removed her panties, she'd be writhing on the bed, begging me to touch her.

Now, it was my time to wait, to experience the same impatience I'd made her suffer through.

She eased her blouse off her shoulders and reached behind her to unfasten her bra. As much as I wanted to look, I didn't. I wouldn't until her eyes released mine.

She held out her hand, and I took it, kneeling between her legs when she spread them. "Touch me," she said, pulling my arm until my hand covered her breast. I caught her nipple between two fingers, leaned down, and circled the other with my tongue. "God, I missed these," I groaned, switching to the other breast. Yeah, I was a tit guy. The rest of Jada's body drove me wild, but I always wanted to start with her breasts. She held my head to her, straining until I sucked hard.

"Zin?"

I released her nipple with a pop and looked up at her. "Look at me."

"Yeah?" I said, staring into her eyes.

"No, look at me."

I pulled back, and rather than just look, I leaned down and kissed every scar I now knew she wanted me to see. Between each meeting of my lips and her flesh, I said, "I love you."

Even when I knew she was crying, I didn't stop. Her hand rested on my head, and rather than pulling me closer or pushing me away, she was with me, every scar, every kiss, every word.

I worked my way down from her breasts to her abdomen. When I reached the waistband of the dress pants she wore, I put one hand on either side of her waist and raised my body.

"Do you want this, Jada? Do you want me to unfasten your pants? Do you want to be naked under me?"

She nodded.

"Say it."

"I want you, Zin. I need you."

I kept my eyes on hers while I took off her pants, then her panties. I tossed them to the side and continued to run my lips and tongue down the front of her body. I spread her folds with my fingers and stared at her pussy that I'd thought I'd never see again, taste again, feel the clench of when I thrust my cock inside her. I pressed my finger to her clit, kept it there, and looked up at her. "You're mine, Jada. If we do this, if I lick you, fuck you with my tongue and cock, you're mine. Do you understand?"

"I'm yours, Zin."

I licked her then, kissing and nibbling what was mine, what would be mine forever. She'd just said it, and I planned to hold her to it.

I slid one finger in deep, and she writhed. I added a second and put pressure on her clit with the pad of my thumb. Jada cried out and arched her back. As much as I wanted to watch her fall apart from just my fingers and mouth, I needed more. I needed to be buried deep in her pussy when she came.

Before I could grab my cock, Jada did. She swirled the tip with her finger.

"I can't wait," I pleaded as much as groaned. She wrapped her hand around my hardness and squeezed. My eyes rolled back in my head. "Jada, *please.*"

"Look at me."

I raised my eyes, straining to keep them open while she stroked me.

"I need to tell you something."

I nearly bit my tongue. *"Now?"*

"Zin?"

"Yeah?" God, couldn't she see how I was hanging on by the skin of my teeth? Any second now, I'd come in her hand, and that wasn't where I wanted to be. Needed to be.

"Are you paying attention?"

If it didn't mean moving away from her pussy, I'd kiss the smug look off her face. "Yes," I said through gritted teeth. "You have my undivided attention."

Her eyes darted back and forth between mine. "I love you." She positioned my cock at her entrance, and I eased rather than thrust inside her. She loved me, and I loved her, and that's what our coming together was all about. *Love.*

With both of us teetering so precariously on the edge, I moved in and out of her slowly, trying to draw it out as long as I could, but when her pussy clenched, I couldn't any longer. I came with a roar before slamming my mouth against hers. I needed to feel her passion, know this meant as much to her as it did to me. Our tongues danced and swirled, teeth nipped, and we both smiled. I eased from her body and lay at her side, unable to stop touching her. I trailed my fingers over her nipples, squeezing, then swirling. Her back arched, but she grabbed my hand.

"Too sensitive," she moaned.

"Too bad," I teased, leaning forward to capture one between my lips.

We made love twice more before Jada snuggled up against me in that way she did right before she fell asleep. I lay, staring at the ceiling for a few minutes, until her soft snores confirmed she was out, then I gently eased out from under her body. I'd heard my cell going off, both with calls and texts, but I'd ignored it. When it buzzed again, I grabbed it and walked out of the room, closing the door behind me as quietly as I could.

"Yeah?" I answered.

"It's Brix. Everyone's been trying to reach you—"

"Tough shit. I've been with the only person who matters. The rest of you assholes can wait."

"I just wanted you to know, the guy who was in the office with Jada is in critical condition. He's in surgery now."

"I gotta tell you, Brix, I really don't give a shit. He had Jada locked in that office. I wouldn't even care if he died.

"That's the thing. e was unarmed."

"Crosby?"

"The man in the office with Jada."

"The door was locked."

"Zin, you can argue with me all you want, but it won't change the fact an unarmed man was shot."

"What do you want from me, Brix? I can't go back and change what happened."

"Vader wants to interview Jada."

"No fucking way."

"I get you want to protect her from this, but Vader may be forced to get a warrant if she won't cooperate."

"I'll talk to her and call you back."

I ended the call and returned to the bedroom. Jada was propped up on her elbows, the sheet pulled up to her chin. "What's going on?"

"Nothing for you to worry about," I said, pulling the sheet down to her waist.

"Zin!" she exclaimed, trying to grab it from my hand.

"Nope. No covering yourself when it's just you and me. That's always been the rule. And if I remember correctly, you were the one who came up with it in the first place. Your exact words were—and I remember them verbatim—'If I'm here, you're naked.'"

She rolled her eyes, but the smile left her face. I crowded her, moved her long hair out of my way, and kissed from beneath her ear, down her neck. I was a breath away from covering her nipple with my lips when she pushed my head.

"I heard you talking in the hallway. Whatever it is, you need to tell me."

I rolled to my back, looked up at the ceiling, and groaned. I knew Jada. She wasn't going to let this go. "What happened earlier? In the office?"

"What do you mean?"

"Who was that guy? What did he say, err, do to you?"

"Nothing. That's why I didn't understand why you broke the door down. I was just about to open it."

"Why was it locked?"

She folded her arms. "Before I answer any more of your questions, tell me what's wrong."

"He was shot."

Jada gasped.

"Apparently, he was unarmed."

She sat up. "*Of course he was unarmed.* He was my ninth-grade science teacher!"

"Whoa, whoa, whoa! Back up, baby. Start at the beginning."

"I was in the office, getting the auction sheets ready, when there was a knock at the door."

"What happened next?"

"Mr. Crosby asked about getting a paddle. I thought he meant for the bachelor auction—"

"Seriously?"

"No, and if you want me to tell you what happened, you have to stop interrupting me."

I nodded and motioned for her to go on.

"At first, I didn't recognize him, but he said he thought I might've been one of his students. Anyway, he thought there were other things being auctioned. Not just bachelors. That's why he was looking for a paddle."

"Why was the door locked?"

"I don't think he meant to lock it. He might've accidentally hit the button. We started talking, and I guess I lost track of time. Like I said, I was about to open the door when the Incredible Hulk broke it down."

"Why'd you scream?"

"I just told you. I was about to open the door. The next thing I knew, Jaicon had a gun pointed at me."

"Jesus," I mumbled, looking up at the ceiling.

"What did you think was happening?"

I closed my eyes, knowing I had to answer her honestly, as much as I didn't want to. "K19 believed someone associated with Varilla and Al Zaabi might be at the auction. That's what Jaicon was doing there, along with the other guy you saw."

"Shit," she muttered.

"It was Brix I was talking to earlier. He said the sheriff wants to question you about what happened."

"Vader?"

I nodded.

"Why does he want to question me?"

"I don't know, maybe because Crosby was unarmed when Jaicon shot him. He'll want to confirm you were in danger at the time."

"But I wasn't. At least I didn't think I was."

"I get that."

She brought her fingers to her mouth and chewed on one of her nails. I grabbed her wrist and stuck that same finger in my mouth instead. "Stop it!" She pulled her finger out of my mouth and started to laugh, but didn't. "So what am I supposed to tell them?"

"The truth, Jada. All you can do is tell the truth."

"What's going to happen to Jaicon?"

I answered truthfully like I told her to. "I have no idea, baby."

35

Jada

Zin asked Brix if Vader could come to the house. Before he arrived, a few of my cousins and Zin's friends, who I knew had been at the event, showed up. Everyone but Tryst. Before they were even in the house, my cell rang with a call from Luisa.

"Are you okay?"

"I'm fine," I quickly assured her. "However, Mr. Crosby was shot."

"I heard. Wasn't he—"

"Our science teacher."

"That's right. He was kind of a weird guy, right? I mean, am I remembering wrong?"

"No, he was weird. At least back then." After he reminded me who he was and we'd started to chat, I just thought he seemed lonely—not dangerous.

"Press wants to know if you want us to fly down."

I looked up at Zin, who was standing close enough to hear our conversation. He shook his head. "Tell her we'll call back after we talk to Vader." The doorbell rang. "That's probably him now."

"I heard," said Luisa. "Call me when you're finished."

I ended the call and met Zin in the living room, where the guys were standing around the room, looking more like mafioso than winemakers.

"Is Vader here?" I asked Zin.

"Sorry, that was just us," said my cousin Kick, pointing to his brother Snapper. I knew there were two years between them, but they looked more like twins. Seeing them made me miss my brothers—and my sisters—not to mention my mom.

When Tryst, Alex, and I arrived from Mexico, I'd gone to stay with her and her husband, Maddox, at their vineyard estate. Demetrius was about twenty miles due west from Zin's place. I'd remained there until shortly before the auction, which meant none of my family, except my cousins, even knew I was here.

Zin put his arm around my shoulders, leaned in, and whispered, "What's wrong?"

"My mom doesn't know I'm in town."

He rested his head against mine. "Maybe we should visit once we're done here."

"We?" Zin had never once suggested the two of us spend time with my family. Or his, for that matter.

"We're not hiding anymore, Jada. Not from anyone." He leaned in and was about to kiss me when the doorbell rang.

Vader was only at the house for fifteen minutes. In that time, he'd asked me the same questions ten different ways. Each time, I answered honestly. No, I hadn't felt threatened by Mr. Crosby, but yes, we were in a locked room.

"Were you present when Ms. Heart shouted at Mr. Crosby to freeze?" he asked.

I vaguely remembered hearing her shout at him, but by that time, Zin had me in his arms and we were exiting the room. "I heard her, but that's all. I didn't see or hear whatever happened after that."

Vader turned to Zin. "Why did you remove Jada from the room?"

"I believed her life was at risk."

"That's all for now," said Vader, standing. Zin walked him to the door.

Once he was gone, I turned to Brix. "What's going to happen to Jaicon?"

"I believe they'll make a decision on whether or not to charge her."

I hated to think they would. However, Zin was right. I couldn't lie. I had to be completely honest. I had no reason to believe Mr. Crosby was a threat to me.

"I should call Luisa back." I excused myself from the room. As I was walking away, I overheard Brix ask Zin if we planned to leave. I turned around when Zin said he didn't know.

"Leave where?"

Zin walked over to me and motioned to the other room. "Let's talk in there."

"Why would we leave?" I asked.

"I don't know all the details, but as I told you before, the K19 team believes there are associates of Varilla and Al Zaabi operating in the area."

"So you think we should leave?"

"I do." He raked his hair with his hand. "I gotta be honest, Jada. The idea that anything could happen to you—" His voice broke, and I put my arms around him.

"I'd say we could go to Mexico, but I should probably talk it over with Tryst first."

Mexico. The meditation center. My room. God, we had so much to talk about. I threw my arms around him and kissed him hard. "I love you so much."

He leaned back and studied me.

"Tryst gave me your letter. Alex was there. Not when he gave it to me. Well, she was, but not in the room with me. Anyway, when I told her I thought it might be too late for us, she talked me into bidding on you at the auction."

"Why didn't you want me to know you were there?"

"Let me see if I can remember how you said it." I lowered my voice, mimicking him. "'I think about you all the time. *All the fucking time*. And I don't really give a shit anymore if you think we don't belong together, because we do, and I'm prepared to prove it to you if you'd just stop pushing me away.' That's why, Zin. Because I was going to prove the same thing to you."

"But that day at Press'…"

"You mean the day you broke up with me?"

"I thought you were breaking up with me."

I shook my head. "You mean when you didn't let me get a single word in?"

"You weren't ending things between us?"

I shook my head again. "I wasn't planning to."

"*Fuck.* All this time, we could've been together…"

"And as awful as that's been, you know what else?"

He shook his head like I had.

"Luisa and Press postponed their wedding."

"When was their wedding?"

"Valentine's Day."

"So, are they married?"

"They're not."

"Fuck," he muttered a second time. He looked down at the floor, then up at me. "We should go to Napa."

"I was thinking the same thing."

Epilogue

Zin

A Month Later

In the days and weeks that followed the Wicked Winemakers' Ball, Alex reported that the final tally of funds raised for the children's hospital was almost twice as much as the year prior, even with the bachelor auction portion of the evening interrupted. I couldn't speak for any of the other *caballeros*, but I gave an anonymous donation, double what I'd brought in the year before. I had no doubt they did as well. It wouldn't have surprised me to learn those not in the auction—like Brix and Press—made donations. too

We hadn't heard anything more about Mr. Crosby other than he survived the surgery. Last I knew, he was still recovering. I also hadn't heard if Jaicon would be charged for shooting him.

Before we left my house, the day of the sheriff's visit, I met with Tomahawk to let him know I'd be gone for an indeterminate amount of time. As we were parting ways, I mentioned how wrong I'd gotten the coyote's lesson.

"You know what they say about spirit animals."

"What's that?"

"Sometimes, they're full of shit."

And here I'd made decisions that could have cost me the one woman I loved more than anything or anyone in the world based on the animal's supposed guidance.

His parting words were ones that would stick with me for the rest of my life. "Follow your own heart, not anyone else's. Trust *your* instincts above all else."

After spending a couple of hours that day with Jada's mom—who hadn't seemed at all surprised to hear her daughter and I had been in a secret relationship, but she'd also insisted no one told her about us—we'd left for Napa, where we stayed with my parents.

Tomorrow morning, we'd fly from here to the airfield at San Luis Obispo, where we'd take a plane large enough to carry all the *caballeros* and our families down to Mexico. A week from now, Press and Luisa would be married. As would Jada and I.

It had been Luisa's idea that we have a joint wedding after she found out I'd proposed. We were reluctant at first, not wanting to take away from their celebration. However, Luisa was as persistent as Press, and the two finally convinced us it was what they wanted more than anything.

"Best friends marrying best friends," Luisa said. "There couldn't be a more joyous celebration."

"You know, I never got to see Rosa's sacred room," I said to Jada once we were on the second plane. "What's it like?"

Jada shrugged. "I haven't seen it either, but Alex has."

"What about Alex?" asked her husband, Maddox, who was sitting a couple of rows in front of us.

"We were talking about Rosa's room in the meditation center. Neither Jada nor I have seen it."

Alex stood and climbed over Maddox's legs. By the time she got to us, her eyes were brimming with tears. "Oh my God, wait until you see it."

"Tell us about it," pressed Jada.

Alex thought for a minute, then shook her head. "Nope, it's something you have to see for yourself."

Keep reading for a
preview of the next book in the
Wicked Winemakers Central Coast
First Label Series,
Tryst's Temptation

**He fought through the pain of his past losses.
She sought healing for her broken heart.
Together, can they find justice and
a love that transcends age?**

TRYST

I never thought I'd find love again after losing my beloved wife to a devastating illness. But when Jaicon Heart walks into my life, everything changes. Despite our age difference, we connect on a soul-deep level. Even when she leaves, I can't let go of hope. I build a house for us, dreaming of a future together. Now, she's back in my arms, and I'll do anything to make her mine forever.

JAICON

After losing my husband and unborn child, I built walls around my heart, convinced vulnerability would only lead to more pain. But Tryst Avila's quiet strength and unwavering support slowly cracked the foundation of my defenses. Even when I ran, his memory followed me into my dreams. Now that we've reunited, I'm finding the courage to heal alongside him. As we work together, fighting human traffickers, I question if my growing feelings are real or just gratitude for his protection. Can I trust myself to recognize genuine love when trauma has reshaped everything I thought I knew about connection?

1

Jaicon

"What do you mean he died?" I gasped. "Sorry. I know what that means, but *he died*?"

"He developed an infection after his surgery that turned into sepsis," Tryst explained in the factual, unemotional way he did when he was talking about something he believed would be traumatic for the person he was speaking with. I'd seen and heard him do it countless times with the people who came to the ranch for equine therapy.

Then I'd loved the way he innately calmed and comforted them. When he did it to me, I hated it.

"My dear Jaicon," he'd begin each time he explained why a relationship would never work between us. It made me want to scream. There were times I'd considered allowing myself to, just to see how the "zen master" reacted.

Today when he knocked on the door of my *casita*, one of many guest accommodations on his ranch in Mexico, it wasn't to tell me what we'd done last night could never happen again. It was to tell me the reason I'd fallen apart, questioned every single thing about myself, had just gotten worse. I hadn't just shot an unarmed man. I'd killed him.

About the Author

USA Today best-selling author Heather Slade writes shamelessly sexy, edge-of-your seat romantic suspense.

She gave herself the gift of writing a book for her own birthday one year. Sixty-plus books later (and counting), she's having the time of her life.

The women Slade writes are self-confident, strong, with wills of their own, and hearts as big as the Colorado sky. The men are sublimely sexy, seductive alphas who rise to the challenge of capturing the sweet soul of a woman whose heart they'll hold in the palm of their hand forever. Add in a couple of neck-snapping twists and turns, a page-turning mystery, and a swoon-worthy HEA, and you'll be holding one of her books in your hands.

She loves to hear from her readers. You can contact her at heather@heatherslade.com

To keep up with her latest news and releases, please visit her website at www.heatherslade.com to sign up for her newsletter.

MORE FROM AUTHOR HEATHER SLADE

ROMANTIC SUSPENSE

K19 Security Solutions Team One
Razor's Edge
Gunner's Redemption
Mistletoe's Magic
Mantis' Desire
Dutch's Salvation

K19 Security Solutions Team Two
Striker's Choice
Monk's Fire
Halo's Oath
Tackle's Honor
Onyx's Awakening

K19 Shadow Operations Team One
Code Name: Ranger
Code Name: Diesel
Code Name: Wasp
Code Name: Cowboy
Code Name: Mayhem

K19 Allied Intelligence Team One
Code Name: Ares
Code Name: Cayman
Code Name: Poseidon
Code Name: Zeppelin
Code Name: Magnet

K19 Allied Intelligence Team Two
Code Name: Puck
Code Name: Michelangelo
Code Name: Typhon
Code Name: Hornet
Code Name: Reaper

K19 Genesis Consortium Team One
Blackjack's Ascent
Dagger's Shield
Sundance's Trail
Nomad's Compass
Preacher's Decree

K19 Sentinel Cyber Team One
Code Name: Admiral
Code Name: Dante
Code Name: Grit
Code Name: Tank
Code Name: Atticus

K19 Sentinel Cyber Team Two
Code Name: Kodiak
Code Name: Paragon
Code Name: Vex
Code Name: Shredder
Code Name: Jagger

Protectors Undercover Team One
Undercover Agent
Undercover Emissary
Undercover Savior
Undercover Infidel
Undercover Shadow

Royal Agents of MI6
Make Me Shiver
Drive Me Wilder
Feel My Pinch
Chase My Shadow
Find My Angel

The Invincibles Team One
Code Name: Deck
Code Name: Edge
Code Name: Grinder
Code Name: Rile
Code Name: Smoke

The Invincibles Team Two
Code Name: Buck
Code Name: Irish
Code Name: Saint
Code Name: Hammer
Code Name: Rip

The Unstoppables Team One
Code Name: Fury
Code Name: Merried

MORE FROM AUTHOR HEATHER SLADE

WINE COUNTRY ROMANCE

BUTLER RANCH
Kade's Worth
Brodie's Promise
Maddox's Truce
Naughton's Secret
Mercer's Vow
Kade's Return
Butler Ranch Christmas

WICKED WINEMAKERS
CENTRAL COAST
FIRST LABEL
Brix's Bid
Ridge's Release
Press' Passion
Zin's Sins
Tryst's Temptation

WICKED WINEMAKERS
CENTRAL COAST
SECOND LABEL
Beau's Beloved
Cru's Crush
Bit's Bliss
Snapper's Seduction
Kick's Kiss

WICKED WINEMAKERS
RUSSIAN RIVER VALLEY
FIRST LABEL
Bas' Blend
Hux's Harvest
Wolf's Want
Oak's Vintage
Cooper's Claim

COWBOY ROMANCE

COWBOYS OF
CRESTED BUTTE
A Cowboy Falls
A Cowboy's Dance
A Cowboy's Kiss
A Cowboy Stays
A Cowboy Wins

ROARING FORK RANCH
Roaring Fork Wrangler
Roaring Fork Roughstock
Roaring Fork Rockstar
Roaring Fork Rooker
Roaring Fork Bridger

SANGRE VISTA RANCH
Thorn's Stand
Stetson's Storm
Maverick's Reckoning
Cinch's Wager
Flints Chance